Trust on Trial

Trust on Trial

G. S. GERRY

RESOURCE *Publications* · Eugene, Oregon

Resource Publications
An Imprint of Wipf and Stock Publishers
199 W. 8th Ave., Suite 3
Eugene, OR 97401

www.wipfandstock.com

PAPERBACK ISBN: 979-8-3852-4689-2
HARDCOVER ISBN: 979-8-3852-4690-8
EBOOK ISBN: 979-8-3852-4691-5

VERSION NUMBER 05/09/25

Contents

Preface

Fool Me Once

SINCE THE DAWN OF TIME, humanity has waged a never-ending battle against life's greatest mind-bending debates. The chicken or the egg? The apple or the banana? Toilet paper: over or under? Sure, they're fun to argue, but at the end of the day, does it really matter?

But what about *the* debates, the ones that split families, shatter friendships, and keep you staring at the ceiling at 3:00 a.m.? Creationism vs. evolution? Pro-life vs. pro-choice? What happens when we die? Is free will an illusion? And yet, of all the age-old questions, one remains the most perplexing, the most dangerous, the most unavoidable: why do we long for trust when betrayal lurks just around the corner?

Trust. We crave it. We build our lives around it. But the moment we grasp it too tightly, it slips through our fingers like we're trying to catch the wind in our hands. They say the path to hell is paved with good intentions, but it's riddled with potholes of misplaced trust that are deep, jarring, and impossible to avoid. The scars of broken trust have inspired sayings passed down from generation to generation:

"Fool me once, shame on you. Fool me twice, shame on me."

"Never put all your eggs in one basket."

"Trust but verify."

Sure, these sayings are clever, memorable. But when has some clever catchphrase insulated our hearts from pain? And yet, despite these warnings, trust infiltrates every aspect of life. It's the invisible currency that fuels friendships, powers institutions, and anchors faith itself. When rightly placed, trust is a stronghold. When misplaced, it leaves us in ruins.

This book begins with a simple yet profound question: *What if Trust could stand trial?*

Let's imagine a packed courtroom. Humanity fills the seats, their hearts burdened with countless stories of betrayal. Every participant undoubtedly has felt the sting of broken trust at some point in their lives. And the defendant? Earnest Trust sits awkwardly at the defense table. He has been arrested and formally charged, and his fate hangs in the balance. Small beads of sweat form on his forehead, and there's an ever-present crease between his brows. His dark hair is freshly cut. A fashionable faded combover is the style for this decade. Lines of exhaustion wrinkled throughout his face tell a story. His bloodshot, heavy eyes scan the room. He's searching, hoping for understanding. He's not looking for sympathy but for sanity. For someone, anyone who gets it. Because this? This is insane.

The initial shock has worn off, but disbelief clings to Earnest Trust like a bad habit. How did he end up here? How did it come to this? How could he be on trial? It's almost laughable, if it weren't so tragic. His wrists, barely visible underneath his shirt cuffs, show circular purple bruising, reminders of the sheer reality of this moment. Around the room, whispers run rampant. Some lean forward, consumed by anger, eager to see Trust convicted, while others hold onto hope and the belief that Trust, when rightly placed, is humanity's only salvation.

So, how did we get here? The truth is simple: we put him here. Humanity is the architect of this moment. Trust has become an object we chase, question, and so often condemn. We forget that the strength of Trust isn't in its nature but in where we place it. And humanity has now taken it one step further, accusing the very thing we so desperately cling to.

As the courtroom files in and the jury takes their seats, the questions loom larger than ever: *Is Trust guilty? Or has humanity placed an impossible burden on something so fragile and fundamental?*

This trial is no ordinary affair. Witnesses from all walks of life line up to testify: a who's who of voices hardened by betrayal, others unshaken by faith, and a mix of everything in between. The prosecution presents a devastating lineup: betrayed lovers, disillusioned employees, the neglected child, an investor robbed of their life savings, the skeptical philosopher, and finally the atheist. Each one is a living testament to Trust's failures.

The defense presents its own lineup: a stark contrast of endurance and resilience, rooted in their convictions, established to inflict layers of reasonable doubt. They have the historian and archeologist, the college students rallying for what's right, the soldier trapped behind enemy lines, and the former atheist turned Christian philosopher. Each of their lives is living proof that Trust, when rightly placed, is the foundation of hope and redemption.

So, stick around; this is just a taste of what's to come.

This trial isn't some boring old lecture; it's an experience. As the trial unfolds, more witnesses will step forward. More evidence will surface. The deeper we go, we'll peel back the layers of history, faith, and humanity's deepest questions.

And when the final gavel strikes? You won't just be watching like some innocent bystander. You'll be forced to decide.

Congratulations, dear reader. You're here to judge. Everyone's favorite pastime. Because you are the jury. You'll sift through the evidence, contemplate the testimonies, and twist under the weight of humanity's deepest wounds as they're paraded around on full display. No pressure, right?

Wrong.

By the end of this trial, you will render the final verdict. But the real kicker? This isn't just about Trust. It's about you—your choices, your letdowns, your situations and circumstances, and ultimately, your future.

In its purest form, Trust is a force of nature, a double-edged sword, a parachute you hope will work when you jump. It's the invisible glue holding the world together, even when it feels like it's slipping through your fingers. We risk it every single day. Sometimes it holds. Sometimes it shatters. And regardless of how the pendulum swings, we keep on trusting. It's like we have amnesia or short-term memory loss. Maybe we do. Maybe it's stubbornness or hard-headedness. Or maybe we just can't help ourselves.

This trial is a mirror. A reflection of the hurts, pains, and questions we ask ourselves every day:

- Why do we trust?

- Why does it fail?

- And can it ever be restored?

The tension is thicker than a snicker. The stakes couldn't be higher. This trial holds the foundations of faith, love, and the entire human experience in its hands. Are you ready?

Because there's no turning back now.

The trial of Trust is here. The jury is called. The evidence awaits. What will you decide?

Introduction

Opening Statements

WELCOME TO THE STAGE for the greatest show on Earth. Justice for all.

Intricately carved, towering double doors stare back at you, daring you to step inside. The dark oak paneling and faded walls are polished just enough to reflect the shifting light. Their height is immense, daunting, mocking the insignificance of each individual passing through.

Crown molding wraps around the room. Its intricate carvings resemble vines or maybe chains, depending on your perspective. Situated at the front of the courtroom is the judge's bench. A throne of authority. Elevated to command the room. The sounding block is a testament to the relentless pounding of gavels past.

Hanging prominently behind the judge's bench are the Ten Commandments. Etched in cold, unyielding stone. It's a constant reminder of the battle between right and wrong. Permanent. Unchanging. Always watching.

There's an aged off-white hue looking down on you from the vaulted ceiling. It holds the weight of countless verdicts, echoes of shattered lives, and sighs of relief. Light trickles through the frosted glass windows, casting faint patterns across the splintered marble floor.

And in the center lies a grand seal, embedded deep into the foundation. Embossed with the words: "IN GOD WE TRUST." A declaration, a reminder that God's fingerprints are everywhere. Even here, especially here. Woven into the tapestry of justice itself.

The courtroom is standing room only. Every seat is occupied. Whispers swirl from bow to stern. A pen clicks. Someone in the gallery clears their throat. Another person exhales just a little too loudly. Even the bailiff, normally stoic, shifts his weight from one foot to another. Every creak of a chair, every rustle of paper, and every second that ticks by on the antique clock amplifies the tension. Every watchful eye is burning a hole through the defendant seated at the defense table.

There he is. Earnest Trust. The accused. He whispers silently to his defense attorney, awaiting the proceedings to commence. He leans back over and holds his head high. His shoulders rest at ease. He smooths the front of his jacket and lightly brushes the hem of his pants. He rubs his finger across his dark brows before clasping his hands together. He's like a skilled poker player who knows when to hold 'em and when to fold 'em.

Trust is a puzzling figure. Equal parts striking and forgettable. Look at him once, and he seems sincere, warm. The guy you'd spill your deepest, darkest secrets to over coffee. Look again: stone-faced, cold, and distant. Like the Thing from *Fantastic Four*: unreadable, immovable, and impossible to relate to.

And his patchwork suit is confusing chaos. Silk next to burlap. Denim stitched into velvet. The seams don't exactly line up. The fabric clashes in the worst possible way. It's elegant and ugly at the same time. I think the fashionistas call that "trendsetting." Sheer genius. A work of art. A fitting embodiment of a guy like Earnest Trust. Beautiful when it holds; hideous when it breaks.

Earnest Trust has an invisible pull to him. It's like gravity or standing too close to the edge of a cliff, unsure if the ground beneath you will hold . . . or crumble. It makes you want to lean in, while you hang on to his every move.

His arrest? That was the most mundane part of this whole fiasco. Swift and without incident. No resistance. No fighting. But this trial? This is something else entirely. This case isn't about one broken pinky promise or a "Sorry, I forgot to text back." This isn't some petty theft case or a Judge Judy episode screaming over unpaid rent. Oh no. Today, Trust stands accused of *fraud* and *breach of contract*. The People want justice. They're not just seeking financial damages, they want compensation for every broken heart, every shattered dream, and a lifetime of asking, "Why me?" This is the trial of the century. *The People v. Trust.*

And by the time it's over, one thing will be clear. The events that follow will either redeem or destroy Trust.

"All rise," the bailiff announces, his words booming through the courtroom. "The honorable Judge Steele presiding."

Enter stage right, Judge Steele, a domineering figure of unwavering authority. His slicked-back, silver-gray hair doesn't move as he races into the courtroom. His robe billows behind him. His imposing gaze seems to peer into the very souls of the room. He's all business and gets straight to the matter at hand. He raises the wooden gavel and strikes the sounding block with the force of Thor's hammer, silencing the courtroom.

BOOM

Court is now in session.

"Ladies and gentlemen, this is no ordinary trial. Today, Earnest Trust stands accused. Not as a concept or an idea, but as a force having wormed its way into the fabric of our existence. The People charge Trust with two counts: fraud and breach of contract. The prosecution will argue beyond a reasonable doubt that Trust is guilty of those crimes and is unreliable, fragile, and fundamentally dangerous. The defense will argue to the contrary that the fault lies not with Trust but with where and how it is placed."

Judge Steele's gaze sweeps across the room, pinning every juror to their seats. Locking eyes like a heat-seeking missile. "As the jury, your role is paramount. The verdict you render will ripple far beyond this courtroom. It will have a far-reaching impact, affecting the way humanity perceives relationships, faith, and even the divine. The stakes don't get any higher."

He pauses, letting the profound weight press down like an elephant sitting on your chest. "Prosecution, you may begin with your opening statement."

The attorney for the prosecution, Curtis Reed, struts around the courtroom like a peacock. He's in his late thirties and his slicked-back, dark brown hair shines in the courtroom. Not a single hair is out of place. He holds his chin high. His shoulders back. Exuding a holier-than-thou arrogance about him. Acting like he owns the place. And in his mind, he does. Every meticulous detail is about keeping up appearances. And he spares no expense. His navy blue suit is sharp, tailored to perfection. It radiates intimidation and smugness. The kind that whispers, "Look at me, I'm richer than you." His tie is the pigment of blood. A power play that says, "I'm here to win at all costs." Reed's face is straight out of a used car salesman's playbook. Ridiculously cheesy and just shady enough to make you check your pockets. This is a man who's never lost a case and doesn't plan on starting now.

Reed's voice is smooth, polished. Meticulously rehearsed and under control. In Reed's mind, the verdict is a foregone conclusion, and he's just going through the motions. His words are carefully constructed for maximum impact. Every word is precise. Every syllable is pronounced. Every pause is designed to make a point. Every hand gesture resembles a maestro conducting a symphony of manipulation. And the jury is his audience.

Curtis Reed rises slowly, adjusting his cufflinks. He steps forward, unhurried. Each measured step lets the silence hang a little more, as his expensive shoes echo to the beat of his drum. Reed is a walking ego trip, and the jury eats it up. He stops just short of the jury box, adjusts his tie, buttons his jacket, and addresses the jury.

"Ladies and gentlemen of the jury, today we put one of the most dangerous defendants in history on trial. Earnest Trust is so fundamental, so universal, that he has touched every single person in the courtroom.

Reed stalks the jury box like a predator. "Trust is a fraud. He egregiously breaches his contracts without any regard for the parties involved. He's a con artist in a suit. He whispers, 'Everything will be okay,' right before yanking the rug out from under you. He smiles, lulling you to sleep before a nightmare shakes you awake in a panic. And we let him. Over and over again.

"But today, we say, no more! Trust is not just fragile; he's dangerous. Trust is an invitation to heartbreak, betrayal, and pain. Trust manipulates us into believing in systems, in people, and even in a God who cannot or will not live up to the demands. And each and every one of you have paid a hefty price."

Reed theatrically pauses before raising his voice. "Let me remind you, you are not just the jurors here. You are the victims. Trust has wronged every one of you. You've trusted friends who've stabbed you in the back. You've trusted employers who've tossed you aside. You've trusted in institutions that have failed you. And you've trusted promises that evaporated into thin air. And for what? For heartbreak? For betrayal? For lost opportunities? For sleepless nights? Wondering, 'Why did I believe their lies?'

"Today, we charge Trust with two counts.

- *Fraud:* For deceiving humanity into believing it is reliable.

- *Breach of Contract:* For failing to deliver on its promises of safety, security, and connection.

"And we are seeking damages that fit these heinous crimes. Compensation for every broken heart, every lost opportunity, and every sleepless night."

While Reed delivers his opening statements, Trust listens intently. If he feels accused, he doesn't show it. He's motionless, under control. No flinching, no frowning, no subtle hints of guilt, no rolling of the eyes. Just a quiet resolve.

It must be irritating Reed because he doesn't like that. Not one, little, bit.

"Ladies and gentlemen, you will hear testimonies from people whose lives were shattered by misplaced Trust. You'll hear from children abandoned by their parents, friends betrayed by those closest to them, and employees discarded by the companies they sacrificed daily for. We will present exhibits that illustrate how Trust doesn't lead to freedom, but despair. Trust isolates us behind walls of fear and handcuffs us to the desk. And these are not isolated incidents. They show a dangerous pattern."

Reed turns and points his bony index finger right at the defendant. "Look at the defendant. Are we supposed to feel sorry for him? He's an arrogant and pompous manipulator. He's left every single one of us broken and abandoned. And now he wants to pretend that he's somehow the victim in all this."

But Trust doesn't back down. He never looks down or away. He meets Reed's glare head-on and dismisses his pointy little finger with intensity. Challenge accepted. He embraces the accusations brought by the prosecution.

The courtroom is so silent you can hear a pin drop.

"And perhaps most damning of all, Trust doesn't just fail in human relationships. The prosecution will prove beyond a shadow of a doubt that Trust, when placed in God's hands, is tested, is dragged to its breaking point, and fails under pressure.

"If God is to be trusted, why does He allow suffering? Why does He permit evil to flourish? Why does He stay silent when people cry out?

"Now, I know you must be asking yourself, 'God? Why are we dragging God into this? What does God have to do with this trial?' It's a fair question. The reason is that Trust and God are inseparable. Intertwined. Tangled together and attached at the hip. Trust isn't just a feeling; it's the foundation for faith itself. If you want to believe in something greater than yourself, what do you need? You need to have faith. Trust forms the basis of faith. Trust is the invisible glue holding every relationship, every belief, every leap of faith together. Make no mistake, God is NOT the one on trial today. Trust is. But we can't ignore this important connection. We can't pretend that one can stand without the other. If we do that, we've already lost.

"Our case is simple: Trust is unreliable and irredeemable. He cannot withstand the weight of human expectations. He breaks, he fails, and he leaves scars that last a lifetime.

"This trial is about more than Trust. It's about you. About your pain, your suffering, your questions, and, ultimately, your future. By the end of this trial, you will have to answer one simple question: Can you afford to Trust anyone or anything again?"

Reed steps back. His voice drops to a whisper. "The case against Trust is just beginning. As we dive further into this case, I want you to ask yourself: Will you continue to place your trust in a defendant that has failed you time and time again? Will you allow this vicious cycle to continue? Or will you render the only verdict that makes sense? GUILTY!"

Reed stops. He takes a moment to look each juror up and down before returning to his seat. His words are like smoke, suffocating the air.

The defense attorney, Harvey Shield, comes into focus. If Reed is a shark . . . sharp teeth, all gas, no brakes, and smells blood in the water, then Shield is a . . . NO, not a minnow. We aren't playing sharks and minnows. Shield is more like a dolphin—intelligent, curious, bold. He's the embodiment of being cooler than the other side of the pillow. He's older than Reed, in his late fifties. His hair is freshly cut and parted to the side with silver and brown expertly mixed together. His suit is a modest, charcoal gray that hangs off his body and poofs out in all the wrong places. His dark leather belt holds up pants that are two sizes too big. His tie is like a clear sky after a rainy day. It's a soothing display of subtlety. Where Reed is swagger and showmanship, Shield is no-nonsense.

Shield's face wrinkles and droops artfully, showing signs of some battles lost and others won, each one inflicting a personal toll. Shield's piercing blue eyes are x-rays that cut through the theatrics, searching for the truth. His voice is smooth. He doesn't rush and never seems to hurry. He has an uncanny ability to make complex arguments sound simple, relating to the jurors on a personal level.

Shield doesn't need theatrics. He doesn't shout and wave his arms like he's flagging down a 747. His words do the talking. Reed is unquestionably the offensive weapon and Shield is the armor, the barrier between his client and the barrage of ammo fired by the enemy.

Harvey Shield rises slowly. He adjusts his tie, buttons his jacket, and steps toward the jury.

"Wow. That was . . . a lot. Reed really knows how to put on a show, doesn't he? The passion. The drama. If this lawyering thing doesn't work out, he's got a career in Broadway waiting for him.

"In all seriousness, ladies and gentlemen of the jury," Shield takes a moment to look each juror in the eyes. "Trust sits before you today as the defendant—not as a heated debate for philosophy class but as a real person accused of actual crimes."

Shield steps back, placing a hand in his pocket. "The prosecution has leveled serious charges against Trust. Fraud. Breach of contract. These are big words with severe consequences. Let's examine these charges more closely, shall we?

"Fraud? The prosecution claims Trust deceives us. Promising safety and connection only to deliver pain and betrayal. But deception is not inherent to Trust. Trust cannot give what it does not have. Deception comes from those who abuse Trust, from those who manipulate Trust for their own self-interest. Trust is not a fraud. Trust is not a con artist. Trust is a gift, a gift we far too often take for granted, misuse, and abuse at our own peril."

Shield lets the jury stew on that for a moment.

"Breach of contract? The prosecution argues that Trust cannot deliver on its promises. But what promises are we talking about? Trust isn't a contract. It's an agreement involving two parties. The problem is that we place our Trust in people and systems that were never meant to carry that type of weight. Only one can bear the full burden of that weight without failing. Only one is worthy of our confidence. And that is God Himself.

"Before we move on, I just want to take a moment to touch on something the prosecution mentioned. Because, folks, did you catch what Mr. Reed said? He brought up faith. He brought up God. He made the connection between Trust, faith, and God. And he is absolutely right. You cannot talk about Trust without talking about God and vice versa. Trust is woven into every relationship we have, and faith is no different. Faith is only as strong as where you place it.

"Throughout this case, the truth will show what happens when you place Trust in the wrong hands and what happens when you place Trust in the right ones.

"The prosecution has painted a grim picture, hasn't he? Trust is a con artist. A losing hand. A house of cards ready to collapse at a moment's notice. He is a threat to society and a danger to us all."

Shield leans in like a space invader. "What the prosecution expertly forgot to mention is that Trust is none of those things. Trust isn't the villain here. He's the patsy, the scapegoat, the source of blame because people hate holding themselves accountable."

Shield motions towards the defendant. "And isn't that the truth? People have used and abused Earnest Trust. He's endured every trial, every betrayal, every lie, every broken promise right alongside each of us. And yet, he still shows up. He still reaches out. He still fights for connection. I call that endurance. Resilience."

As Shield pleads his argument, Trust shifts in his chair. He leans forward slightly, staring at the jury. He purses his lips together and tightens his clasped hangs. Trust scans the jury, looking like he wants to speak, to explain himself, to tell his side of the story. But he can't. Now is not the time.

Shield continues. "Ladies and gentlemen, don't allow the prosecution to mislead you by pulling at your heartstrings. The prosecution wants to convince you that Trust is inherently broken. But Trust is vital. The prosecution wants to focus on the negative aspects of Trust and lock away all of the positives. There are two sides to every story, two sides to every coin. Trust is not the criminal here. He is a mirror. When placed in the right hands, Trust reflects stability, hope, and life-changing connection. When placed in the wrong hands, Trust reflects human weakness, misplaced priorities, and the pain of betrayal.

"And that's the real issue, isn't it?

"We place our trust in all the wrong things. We Trust in flawed people, in failing systems, in fleeting ideas. And when they let us down? We don't blame ourselves. Instead, we have to blame something else, someone else. So, what do we do? We shift the blame onto someone else, and today, that someone is Earnest Trust.

"But let me ask you. Is it fair to blame the foundation for the cracks in a poorly built house?" Shield shakes his head. "Trust is the foundation of love, connection, and faith. Without Trust, we become isolated, suspicious, and fearful. Yes, misplaced Trust can lead to pain. But rightly placed Trust is unshakable, unbreakable, and transformational."

Shield slowly sweeps his hand across the jury, taking a personal tone. "When you cross a bridge, do you blame the act of walking if the bridge collapses? Or do you blame the builder? Trust is the act of crossing the bridge. Because Trust is not the problem, the bridge is. The prosecution will show you failed bridges. Betrayals. Corruption. Failing institutions. False promises. On and on and on down the line. All in an attempt to say, 'Look! Do you see what Trust did? Trust is dangerous. Trust is a lie. Off with its head.'

"But the answer isn't to abandon Trust. When we get knocked down, the right response is to get back up again. The answer is obvious. Why not build stronger bridges? Why not place our Trust where it belongs, in the hands of one who never fails? The answer is the Most High God who never fails and is completely trustworthy.

Shield looks across the sea of jurors. "This trial isn't about abandoning Trust. It's about asking the right question. Have we been placing our Trust in the wrong things all along?"

Pausing, he allows the jury time to truly consider the question. "Ladies and gentlemen, the prosecution wants you to condemn Trust. They'll scream that a verdict of guilty is the only option, that you must lock Trust away forever in the prison of your doubts and throw away the key. They want you to let your pain dictate your decision. But isn't that manipulation?

"But we will show you the truth. We will present undeniable proof to the contrary. We will call witnesses who have endured unimaginable hardships and found healing, hope, and renewal through Trust. And why is that? It's because they placed their Trust in the right hands. This is not a myth. This is not a theory. These are the facts.

"This is a defense built on sound logic and reasoning, on irrefutable evidence, and ultimately, on the truth. I'm here to challenge you. Don't let the failures of flawed people and flawed systems rob you of the freedom that comes from placing your trust in the right hands, in the one who never fails.

"Ladies and gentlemen of the jury, this trial is not just about the fate of Trust. It's about your future, your heart, your soul. And by the time this trial is over, the choice will be abundantly clear. You, the jury, will issue a resounding verdict of NOT Guilty.

"Thank you."

Mic drop.

Shield walks back to his seat, slightly nodding his head and winking in the direction of Earnest Trust.

The opening statements have been delivered. The battle lines are drawn. And now, the real fight begins.

The prosecution has a mountain of witnesses with stories so gut-wrenching, so heartbreaking even the Grinch's heart would ache. They have betrayal, heartbreak, and disappointment at their ever beck and call. They'll pile it on thick, shouting from the rooftops that Trust is guilty beyond a shadow of a doubt. Trust has failed you, lied to you, and left you for dead.

But the defense will counter with a calculated witness list of their own. People who had every reason to walk away from Trust forever. People who were betrayed. People who were broken. People who should've given up. People who should've just stayed down for the ten count. But they didn't. Instead, they found something else. They found resilience, redemption, and unshakable hope.

And let's not forget the exhibits in this trial. Tangible, cold, hard evidence of Trust's impact on the world. It cuts both ways, leaving a lasting impression. On one side, it's damning. Brutal. An open-and-shut case of deception, betrayal, and a lifetime of Trust's failures. The other side? Kicking and screaming redemption, itching for a second chance. And neither side is going down without a fight.

The prosecution will try to bury Trust under an avalanche of proof. They'll show you the scars, the shattered lives, the empty promises, the unequivocal guilt of Trust through and through. Exhibit A? The forbidden fruit. The apple from Eden. The moment the silver-tongued charlatan, the serpent, eroded the foundation of perfect trust by planting a seed of doubt. "Did God really say . . . ?"

Exhibit B? Judas's thirty pieces of silver. The OG Benedict Arnold. This cold, metallic symbol carries the weight of ultimate betrayal. And that's just the appetizer. The prosecution will lay it on thick. Each exhibit is carefully designed to paint Earnest Trust as a villain, a loaded gun.

But the defense? They'll fight to plant seeds of doubt. They'll present evidence of historical fact and undeniable truth that Trust is not guilty on all counts. "The first one to plead his cause seems right, until his neighbor comes and examines him" (*Proverbs 18:17*).

The defense will present evidence such as the Foundation Stone in Jerusalem, believed to be the site where Abraham was prepared to sacrifice Isaac, trusting in a promise that made no sense. This monument is where faith defined history. Then there's the Babylonian artifacts confirming King Nebuchadnezzar's reign, undeniable proof that the fiery trial of Shadrach,

Meshach, and Abed-Nego isn't just the stuff of legend but historical fact. Then there's the Cross, the ultimate portrayal of sacrifice, trustworthiness, and redemption. Each exhibit introduces layers of reasonable doubt designed to open your eyes and see Earnest Trust as he is: a victim, a scapegoat, an easy target to blame for humanity's Trust issues.

And the truth of the matter is that Trust is a puzzle. It's up to the jury to decide which pieces fit together. Some will see him as a hero who carried them through their darkest nights. Some will see him as a traitor, a Benedict Arnold, a master manipulator who lured them into disaster. And others? They'll see something else entirely. A reflection.

And now, it's up to you. Because this is personal. Are you ready to step into the jury box and confront your own doubts, your own pain, and your deepest questions? Every betrayal, every broken promise, every moment you've hesitated to trust again all comes down to this.

You'll see the evidence. You'll hear the testimonies. And when it's all said and done? You, the jury, face the most difficult decision of all. The final verdict rests in your hands. So, what will it be?

Let the truth be revealed. Let the arguments unfold. Let the verdict be delivered. *The People v. Trust begins now.*

CHAPTER 1

The Prosecution Attacks

THE WORLD IS WATCHING. They're waiting to see what you'll do. This is the trial. This case will define a generation. Whatever you decide will be analyzed, debated, and whispered about in conversations for decades to come. And your fingerprints will be all over it. It's only your legacy on the line. No pressure, right?

So here's the real question: Are you the hero? The one willing to defend Trust? Or are you the villain? The one ready to condemn Trust to the electric chair? Savior or executioner?

Can you feel it? The pulse throbbing in your neck. The tension in your chest. The air is electric. Judgment hangs heavy, suffocating the courtroom like an overused cologne that's worn out its welcome. The gallery is swirling with curiosity, doubt, and suspicion. The whole courtroom is on the verge of exploding. And in strolls Curtis Reed. The prosecution's golden boy, strutting around like a rooster at sunrise. His briefcase snaps open like a declaration of war.

"All rise," the bailiff announces.

The defendant, Earnest Trust, slowly stands. Wrinkles cover his suit, and his tie is slightly uneven. He's probably adjusted it a dozen times but never quite got it right. He scans the room from front to back. He looks tired, his eye lids heavy and his eyes clouded with red. He has a look of, "I've been through worse, but this sucks."

"Is the prosecution ready to present their case?" Judge Steele's voice booms.

"We are, Your Honor."

Brace for impact.

Reed rises, buttons his jacket, and saunters toward the bench. He smirks as he dives in. His tone is sharp, slicing through the heavy silence. All eyes are trained on the cocky counselor.

"Ladies and gentlemen of the jury, Trust is not what it seems. It's not the sturdy pillar we've been led to believe. It's a house of cards. Today, we argue Trust is unreliable and a liability. It's a risk too dangerous to take. And we are here to hold Trust accountable for the real damage he has caused."

"Trust stands accused of fraud and breach of contract. These are serious crimes that have left countless lives in ruins. He has shattered lives, broken hearts, and crippled futures. And we will show that Trust is not your ally. He is the enemy. He is a con artist, a master of deception of the highest order."

Reed looks around the room, silent, letting the words sink in. "The evidence will show that Trust is a liar, a thief, and a destroyer. He makes promises he cannot keep. Today, you will see the true face of Trust, a face of guilt.

"And let me remind you. You're not just the jurors, you're the victims. You've been lied to, cheated, abandoned. Today, we take back control. Today, we hold Trust accountable.

"Let's begin with the first charge: *fraud*. Fraud is the intentional deception of another for personal gain OR to cause harm. A lie told with purpose. And time and time again, Trust has proven to be a resourceful liar, misleading us to confide in him and taking advantage of that kindness."

Reed's lips curl as he points to the defendant. "We'll start with the defendant's character, shall we? The very definition of Trust. What is Trust, really? Why do we rely on him? And why does he keep failing us?

"Your Honor, I'd like to introduce our first exhibit into evidence." The bailiff steps forward, placing a polished apple on the evidence table. It gleams under the courtroom lights, a symbol both simple and profound. (Honestly, it looks more ready for an Instagram post than a critical piece of evidence for utter betrayal.)

"This," Reed mockingly examines every inch of the apple, "is *Exhibit A: The Apple from Eden*. A fruit so innocent, so tasty, I'd like to take a big, juicy bite right about now. Is it lunchtime yet?"

A few laughs echo through the courtroom.

"This is where it all started. This apple represents the first great betrayal of Trust in all of human history."

Reed hoists the apple high. "In the Garden of Eden, Trust was pure, whole, unbroken. Adam and Eve trusted God completely, and he trusted their obedience. But then came the serpent. A liar. A deceiver. A sower of doubt. All he had to do was whisper four simple words, 'Did God really say ...?' (Genesis 3:1)

"And just like that," *CRACK!* Reed slams his hand on the jury box. "At that exact moment, Trust cracked. Eve trusted the serpent, and Adam followed suit. And what was the result? Catastrophe. Trust was shattered in the blink of an eye. And we have felt the aftershocks of that betrayal ever since. It's the reason we're all here today."

Reed sets the apple back down on the table. With the apple in full view, gleaming on the table, Reed pivots to the screen behind him. He dramatically clicks, and the screen in front of the jury flashes. The definition of Trust appears in bold letters.

Trust

1. (n.) Assured reliance on the character, ability, strength, or truth of someone or something.

2. (n.) A dependence on something future or contingent as if it were present or certain.

3. (n.) That which is entrusted to another, something given in confidence.

4. (v.) To place confidence in; to rely on or entrust with responsibility.[1]

Reed gives the jury time to read. With phony sincerity, he approaches.

"Trust," Reed drags out the word, "is belief. It's confidence placed in someone or something. It's the belief, the hope that what we expect to happen will come to pass. It's the pillar of every relationship. It's in every decision we make and every hope we've ever had. But what happens when that pillar cracks and gives way? As you will see, people often misplace this belief, leading to pain, betrayal, and brokenness."

Reed clicks and the screen shifts. More words and definitions appear:

Confidence

1. (n.) Faith or belief that one will act in a right, proper, or effective way.

2. (n.) A relation of trust or intimacy.[2]

---

1. (Merriam-Webster.com Dictionary, s. v. "trust" 2024)
2. (Merriam-Webster.com Dictionary, s. v. "confidence" 2025)

Entrusting

1. (v.) To commit to another with confidence.
2. (v.) To confer a trust on; to give over responsibility.[3]

"Confidence," Reed clasps his hands together, "is the foundation of trust. It's the feeling of certainty that what we believe will hold true. And entrusting? This is the act of handing over something precious. Maybe your heart, maybe your safety, or maybe even your future to someone else. But here's the problem: when confidence falters, when entrusting goes off track, the fallout is disastrous."

Another click, another shift.

Reed doubles-down, linking trust to its closest relative: belief.

"Trust is fundamentally about belief. To believe in someone or something is to also trust them, to have faith that they will not fail you. But here's the problem: people often misplace belief, just as they misplace trust. So, why are we going through this grammar exercise? Who cares? Well, we do. We care. Because Trust, belief, and confidence are all connected. To understand the significance of Trust, we need to know the impact it has in our lives."

Reed clicks one last time and a strange-looking word appears. *Pisteuō*

Reed squints at the screen. "Now, let's all take a moment to appreciate this beautiful Greek word: *pist-*"

He tries to sound it out.

"Piss . . . taco? Pissed . . . two?" He scratches his head. "You know what? Let's just call it 'pistachio.' Kinda rolls off the tongue, doesn't it?"

A few chuckles flow through the courtroom. Even Judge Steele smirks.

Reed grins, crossing his arms. "I know, I know. First, it was grammar time; now, we're learning a foreign language. What gives? Well, this fancy little word *pisteuō* [4] for belief means to have faith, to entrust oneself to another. Sounds comforting, doesn't it? But do you see the danger here? Do you see the predicament that puts you in? Trust requires us to hand over a piece of ourselves, to risk everything. And if we're being honest, it fails us most of the time.

"The question remains, is Trust worthy of that risk? Or is it just one big, overpriced bag of pistachios . . . full of empty, disappointing shells?"

Reed lets the jury stew on it for a moment.

3. (Merriam-Webster.com Dictionary, s. v. "entrusting" 2024)
4. (Bible Hub.com, 4100. Pisteuo, 2024)

The bailiff steps forward again with an expression of, "Why so serious!?" This time? He's carrying a small burlap bag.

CLINK. The sound cuts through the courtroom as it drops onto the evidence table.

Reed moseys on over, raising the bag like a magician about to reveal a trick. "*Exhibit B,*" giving the bag a shake as the coins collide, jingle-jangling together. "Sounds like there's about thirty pieces of silver in here. Don't you think?"

The jury sits up straight. Most everyone knows this story. They know where this is heading.

Reed smirks. His polished shoes tap in a steady rhythm against the floor, each step measured, deliberate. "This symbol marks one of history's greatest betrayals. Thirty pieces of silver. The price of Trust sold out. Judas Iscariot. The man, the myth, the world's most infamous backstabber. Benedict Arnold's role model.

"He was one of Jesus' twelve disciples. A guy who walked with him, learned from him. Judas even broke bread with him. This is a man who called Jesus 'Teacher.' And for what?" Reed violently shakes the bag again. "A handful of silver."

He tosses the bag onto the table next to the apple. The two exhibits form a one-two punch of betrayal.

"Let that sink in for a second." Reed leans in, whispering, "If Jesus himself, the embodiment of truth and love, could be betrayed, what hope do the rest of us have? You don't think your best friend would sell you out for the right price? Your business partner? Your spouse?"

Reed shrugs, placing one hand in his pocket. "This bag proves one simple truth. Trust is deadly."

Deafening silence.

The jury shifts and looks at one another. At the defense table, Earnest Trust lets out a deep, slow sigh. He rubs his thumb and index finger slowly between his smile lines. He grabs a pen and scribbles something on the yellow legal pad in front of Shield. Shield furrows his brows, shakes his head, and writes, "It's ok!" underneath Trust's note. Circling it.

The placement of the coins next to the apple creates a tableau of broken trust that speaks louder than words.

Reed pulls out his little clicker and the screen shifts. This time, it's a timeline labeled *Exhibit C*: The Hall of Broken Trust:

1. The Garden of Eden: Humanity's first betrayal.

2. Judas Iscariot: Trust sold for silver.

3. Modern Times: Corporate fraud, The Bernie Madoff Ponzi Scheme, political scandals, and institutional failures.

Reed points to the timeline. "This isn't just history, folks. It's evidence." Reed smirks, tapping a file in front of him. Then he drops the hammer.

"The People present *Exhibit D: The Bernie Madoff Ponzi Scheme*."

BOOM.

The name ricochets through the courtroom. An indecipherable roar erupts in the gallery.

"Order. Order in the court!" Judge Steele commands, slamming his gavel down.

Jaws tighten. People fume loudly through their noses. Reed lets the tension bubble before continuing.

"Ahh, the infamous Bernie Madoff. The king of con. The Picasso of Ponzi. The man didn't just steal billions. Madoff didn't just empty bank accounts; he emptied lives. His victims? Ordinary people. Teachers, retirees, charities, grandmothers, the list is a mile long. I don't think he ever met a person he wouldn't happily steal from. All these people had faith in him, in the system, in the 'too good to be true' promises that turned out to be, well . . . too good to be true."

He taps the file in front of him. Once. Twice.

"But let's be clear: Bernie Madoff wasn't the only criminal party." He pauses. "Oh no. Madoff had a partner. A manipulative and cunning accomplice enabled this whole charade to go on for decades."

He turns and points right through Earnest Trust.

"That accomplice? That co-conspirator? That enabler of ruin was none other than Earnest Trust."

GASP!

"It was Trust that convinced those victims to part with their life savings. It was Trust that whispered, 'This is safe. This is secure. This is the future.'

"And in the blink of an eye?" Reed snaps his fingers. "Gone. Tell me, ladies and gentlemen, when it all came crashing down, who paid the price? Was it Trust? Of course not. No way, Jose. Trust never pays. Trust always gets off scot-free. The victims are the ones left holding the tab. It's the victims that are bankrupt, broken, and destitute. The victims are the ones who put their faith in something that never deserved it. Trust didn't just fail them. It ruined them."

The jury shifts, uncontrollably scrunching and contorting their faces.

And Trust? He's a sneaky statue. Even though he sees the anger in the jury's eyes, he doesn't look away. His eyes dart from one juror to the next, mirroring their suffering and their sorrow.

"Your Honor," Reed announces, adjusting his cufflinks, "the prosecution calls our first witness, Mrs. Sarah Jacobs."

A woman in her sixties steps forward. Her rosy cheeks heavily dabbed with blush invite memories of baking cookies. A clinking from her red and gold stone necklace announces her arrival as she slowly shuffles toward the stand. She's wearing a light red jacket and tan pants. The overhead light catches her blonde and silver-streaked hair, giving her an almost angelic glow. She holds her chin high and moves with a kind authority. She looks around the courtroom with patient, knowing eyes like she's already forgiven you for whatever trouble you've gotten yourself into. Her face is lined with years of care that speaks to a life fully lived. She has no smiles today. Instead, it's replaced by pursed lips and a somber look. She walks into the witness stand, raises her hand, and swears the oath. As she sits, she adjusts a tarnished bracelet on her delicate wrist.

"Can you state your name and occupation for the court?"

"Sarah Jacobs, and I'm an office assistant," she says with a southern drawl.

"Mrs. Jacobs, could you please tell the court about your experience with Bernie Madoff?"

"My husband and I worked our entire lives. We scrimped and saved every penny. We worked late-night shifts, sacrificed constantly. All of it was for our future. Short-term pain for long-term gain is how we looked at it. We wanted security. We wanted to retire. We wanted to help our grandkids through college." She laughs bitterly. "And then we heard about him."

"Bernie Madoff." She spits the name out like a rotten piece of fruit. Bernie Madoff, a name that lives in infamy. Synonymous with a rat. A wolf in sheep's clothing. A well-dressed con artist.

"Mrs. Jacobs, you said you wanted to retire. But earlier, you stated you were an office assistant. What happened?

"When we heard about Madoff's fund, it seemed like the perfect opportunity. Everyone we knew trusted him. He was safe. He had credentials. He had connections. He had Trust." A rush of air escapes from between her lips while she nervously fidgets with her bracelet. "So we invested. Every-thing. And then? We lost it all. Every. Last. Cent. Our dreams of retirement, helping our grandchildren with college? It was all gone."

"Mrs. Jacobs, I couldn't help but notice you playing with your bracelet. Can you tell us about that?

"My granddaughter gave this to me for my birthday years ago. It wasn't expensive, but it's priceless. You know how it is when your grandkids give you something. I don't have any expensive jewelry anymore. I had to sell all that just to make ends meet, once he stole everything from us. And it's a good thing too, because he would've snatched this right off my wrist. That man is a monster. He would literally take the clothes off your back if you let him.

"And it wasn't just about the money. It was the betrayal. We trusted him. We trusted the system. We trusted . . . " she burns a hole in the defen-dant, "Trust. And he destroyed us!"

Her final words drop like a ton of bricks.

And Trust? He cringes. He slouches forward in his chair. He looks down at the table and scrunches his face. Something inside him seems to break a little. If this is how the testimonies are going to go, Trust will be in a hole so deep it'll be nearly impossible to climb out of.

"Objection, Your Honor," Shield interjects, leaping from his seat. "My apologies for interrupting Mrs. Jacobs's testimony. The witness is blaming Trust for the crimes of an infamous con man. Bernie Madoff was a scoun-drel. A fraud. A monster. But to hold the defendant, Earnest Trust, account-able for his deception is unfair. It's like blaming a knife for a stab wound it inflicts. The issue isn't Trust; it's who wields it."

The judge leans back, strumming his fingers. "Overruled for now. But tread carefully, Counselor."

Reed smirks. "Noted, Your Honor. No further questions."

Shield approaches the witness stand. "Mrs. Jacobs, your story is heart-wrenching. I'm disgusted by the thought of anyone taking advantage of my grandmother. I'm sorry for the immense pain this must have caused.

"Mrs. Jacobs, I'd like to clarify something. You said you trusted Bernie Madoff because of his reputation, correct?"

"Yes."

"And that reputation, would you say it was built on lies?"

"Well, yes, I suppose so." Her brow pinches together.

"So, if Madoff acted fraudulently from the start, was it Trust that betrayed you? Or the man you placed your trust in? Is it fair to say that this man manipulated your trust, rather than your trust was misplaced?"

"I . . . I guess that's true."

Shield moves in front of the jury.

"Ladies and gentlemen, let's be clear. Mrs. Jacob's story is horrific. The devastation left behind by a monster like Bernie Madoff is overwhelming. What she endured should never happen to anyone. Ever. But we can't lose sight of who the true villain is here. Trust didn't steal Mrs. Jacobs's life savings. It wasn't Trust that spun lie after lie after lie. It wasn't Trust who schemed, and plotted, and manipulated thousands of innocent men and women like Mrs. Jacobs to give him their life savings.

"It was Bernie Madoff, a truly despicable man who would steal the clothes off your back if you let him. It was Bernie Madoff who misused Trust. Bernie Madoff sits in prison, paying the penalty for his crimes. As horrifying as Mrs. Jacobs's testimony is, we cannot unfairly attach that guilt to the defendant today."

Shield returns to his seat. Reasonable doubt, welcome to the party.

Reed pivots to his next target, flipping through his notes. "Now, ladies and gentlemen, let's talk about the second charge. Breach of contract.

"Trust isn't just some warm and fuzzy feeling. It's in every handshake, every agreement, every contract. Trust is written in the fine print. And when Trust fails, it's not just some 'whoopsie-daisy.' It leaves behind a trail of broken relationships, ruined careers, and shattered lives.

Reed lifts up a contract so thick it reminds the jury of the phone book. "This is *Exhibit E*, the physical symbol of a business deal gone sideways, a livelihood flushed right down the toilet.

"Your Honor, the prosecution calls Mr. Grant Waverly."

The doors swing open and a weary man in his late fifties enters. Grant Waverly's peppered brown hair catches the courtroom's attention. His shoulders slump forward and he walks with a slight limp as his pant leg drags on the floor. His short-sleeved white shirt and gray pants are wrinkled. His eyes dart around the courtroom, careful to avoid eye contact. Grant Waverly settles into the witness chair, gripping the rail to maintain his posture.

"Mr. Waverly, can you please tell the jury what happened when you trusted your business partner?"

"We were supposed to open a restaurant together," Mr. Waverly's voice shakes with his head tilted down. "I put up most of the money. My business partner was supposed to handle the operations side of the house."

"And how did that go?"

"At first, things seemed fine. Then the money started disappearing. He told me it was for expenses, but the math wasn't adding up." Mr. Waverly shakes his head. The sound of his leg bouncing up and down echoes in the microphone.

"And when did you realize what was really going on?"

"When I checked the account, it was empty. Zilch. Zero. Nada. He cleaned me out and skipped town."

"And how did that affect you?"

"I lost everything." Mr. Waverly clenches his teeth, wincing. "My savings. My credit. My reputation. I had to declare bankruptcy. Trust didn't just fail me. It flat-out *ruined* me."

Licks finger and tallys another point for the prosecution.

"And what is your occupation now, Mr. Waverly?"

"I'm a janitor at the local high school."

The jury gasps, whispering amongst themselves.

Trust grimaces as Mr. Waverly describes his current occupation. He can't bear to look up at the jury or the witness, instead focusing on the shades of wood on the table. The pain of Mr. Waverly's circumstances is sickening, causing knots in his stomach. Trust looks ill, green almost. He fidgets in his chair, adjusting his sleeves. As Mr. Waverly describes his devastation, there is a slight droop of Trust's head. Is it an acknowledgment of guilt? Regret? Frustration? Or something more? Only time will tell.

Reed turns to the jury. "You see, this is what happens when you Trust. It's a loaded gun just waiting to go off. It wounds you and leaves you for dead."

"Objection, Your Honor," Shield roars, pointing his finger. "While the witness's testimony is devastating, Mr. Reed is leading the witness to blame Trust itself rather than a person's actions. Trust is a neutral concept. It does not lie, nor does it steal. It is people who misuse Trust—that is the issue here."

Judge Steele rubs his face, tapping his index finger on his chin. "Sustained. Tread lightly, Counselor."

With a passionate tone, Reed confronts the jury. "Ladies and gentlemen, this is precisely the point. Trust is not a neutral party. It's a willing participant. It's always in the room, shaking hands, making deals, and offering false reassurances. Trust is not some innocent bystander. He's an accomplice, a full-blown co-conspirator.

"Think about it. Have you ever been deceived by someone you didn't trust? Of course not!" Reed shouts. "Trust enabled them! Whispering in your ear, 'Go ahead. It's safe. Nothing will happen.' Trust demands that we lower our guard. And when we do, Trust is broken. The fallout is catastrophic. This is precisely why Trust is guilty. Trust is the accomplice to every betrayal, the silent partner in every slick con."

Shield stands and approaches the witness. "Mr. Waverly, you've experienced tremendous loss. I can't sympathize enough with the agony of your situation. Mr. Waverly, how long did you know your business partner?"

"Twenty years. He was more than a business partner; he was my friend. And that's what makes his betrayal so much worse."

"Mr. Waverly, you trusted your business partner, didn't you?"

"Of course I did. We were friends for a long time. We went through a lot together."

"And in those twenty years, did he ever lie to you? Did he ever act in an untrustworthy manner?"

"Yeah, who hasn't? Twenty years is a long time. No one's perfect."

"Mr. Waverly, that's true. No one is perfect. Would you say that your friend betrayed you?"

"Yes."

"Did your friend and business partner steal from you?"

"Yes."

"Mr. Waverly, shouldn't we hold your friend and business partner accountable? Isn't he the person responsible for taking advantage of you?"

"Well, yes, but —"

"And, Mr. Waverly, if the police were able to find your business partner, wouldn't you want him to face the fullest extent of the law?"

"Absolutely."

"So, if that's the case, why are you pointing the finger at Trust? Why are you blaming Trust when your business partner is the one who wronged you? . . . No further questions, Your Honor."

Reed jumps up, "Permission to redirect, Your Honor."

"Proceed."

"Mr. Waverly, has your business partner been located?"

"No," Mr. Waverly frowns, sighing at the injustice.

"If you didn't Trust your business partner, would you have entered into a partnership with him?"

"Haha, of course not. That's the reason to do business with someone. There's a layer of Trust baked in."

"I couldn't agree more. Thank you, Mr. Waverly. No further questions."

Reed takes a step back. "Look at this evidence." He sweeps his hand, pausing on each exhibit. "The apple from Eden. The bag of silver coins. The hall of broken trust. The Bernie Madoff Ponzi scheme. The broken contract.

"These aren't just stories or cautionary tales. These are facts. Indisputable proof of the carnage left behind by Trust's failures."

Reeds starts locking eyes with the jurors. One. By. One.

"Let's be honest with ourselves. Why do we keep doing this? Why do we keep on trusting? Why do we keep placing our faith, our Trust in people, in systems, in things that are guaranteed to fail? Why do we keep falling for the same scam, over and over again? And why on earth aren't we holding the actual culprit accountable?"

Reed crosses his arms as the silence races on.

"Ladies and gentlemen, we are just beginning to understand the extent of Trust's crimes. Tomorrow, we'll go deeper with more witnesses, more betrayals, more undeniable evidence of Trust's criminal actions and liability."

Reed side-eyes Earnest Trust as he struts to his seat. A look that says, "*Game over.*"

Judge Steele slams his gavel, announcing, "Court is adjourned for the day. The jury will remember their admonition. Court will resume at 9 a.m. tomorrow morning."

As Day One concludes, the jury reflects a kaleidoscope of emotions: anger, doubt, and, for some, sympathy for Earnest Trust. Today was like a train wreck, brutal and impossible to look away from.

The prosecutor's words dance circles in the air. The juror's minds swirl with questions: Is Trust irredeemable? Is Trust really the villain they've been led to believe? Or is Trust the fall guy, framed by the people who took advantage of it for their own selfish gain? Has humanity simply been placing it in the wrong hands all along?

With court adjourned, the coffee shop across the street rushes with caffeine addicts and courtroom gossip. Welcome to Jitters Prevail, a café where the espresso machines whistle, the grinders vibrate, and the baristas never spell the customer's name right.

At one table, Curtis Reed lounges in his chair, a persistent smirk splattered across his smug little face. He stirs his coffee with one hand, tapping the other deliberately on the table to the beat of his own drum.

Across the shop, Harvey Shield sits, one leg over the other, in his own little world, ignoring the noise around him. His coffee remains untouched as steam billows from the lid vent. He pretends like he doesn't see Reed, but let's be honest. He sees him.

Reed can't take it anymore. He knows Shield is ignoring him. He races over to Shield like a man possessed. "Shield, you're not fooling anyone. You should quit while you're behind. This case is a slam dunk. Trust's as guilty as sin. I've got the jury eating out of my hand."

Shield nonchalantly looks up, unbothered by Reed's rude interruption.

"Look, I could drag this out. This goes against my better judgment, but I'm feeling generous. Let's end this here and now." Like a magician pulling a rabbit from his hat, Reed slaps the plea agreement down next to Shield's coffee. "Here's the plea deal."

Ta-Daaa

"Fifteen years. Eight with good behavior. This is a good deal, Shield. Don't take long to decide before I change my mind. Remember, I'm throwing you a bone here."

"A bone, you say. Is that what you call it? Funny, it looks more like a casket." Shield squints. "Don't you have something better to do? You know as well as I do, your case is circumstantial at best."

"Circumstantial?" Reed barks. "Were we in the same courtroom? Broken contracts, ruined relationships, betrayals stacked a mile high. You think the jury needs any more than that? The jury always needs someone to blame. And right now, they don't trust Trust. And before it's over, they'll never trust him again."

"And yet . . . here you are." Shield sips his coffee, grinning ever so slightly. "Offering us a plea. Do you smell that?" Shield mockingly sniffs the air. "It smells like desperation."

Reed's eyes open wide.

"If your case was so airtight, you wouldn't be going out of your way to offer us so much as a Tic Tac." Shield picks up the plea deal and glances at it before setting it back down. "You're questioning yourself, Curtis. It's kinda cute."

"Shield, don't be stupid." Reed clenches his jaw. "If this goes to verdict, Trust is done for."

"Oh, I'll present this to my client." Shield slowly rises, his chair scraping against the floor like nails on a chalkboard. "But between you and me, I think the jury's a little smarter than you give them credit for."

Shield takes one last swig of coffee, grabs his briefcase, and heads for the door.

Reed remains seated. The rage inside him intensifies. "We'll see about that," he whispers.

CHAPTER 2

The Blame Game

YESTERDAY WAS DRAMATIC, full of intrigue and legal fireworks. But today? Buckle up, it's gonna be a bumpy ride.

Earnest Trust hunches over in his chair like a one-hundred-pound weight vest is strapped to his chest. His suit is not as crisp today. It's wrinkled, sagging. Even his tie seems to lack confidence, hanging loosely from his neck, worried about strangling him. But his eyes tell the story. Slight bags are starting to show. He looks down and away. The exhaustion of the grueling trial begins to settle in.

Reed struts into the courtroom. His peacock swagger never wavers. He approaches the jury, making uncomfortable eye contact with each of them.

"Ladies and gentlemen, today we further examine the consequences of broken Trust. When trust is betrayed, the human heart cries out, 'Why me? What did I do wrong? Who is to blame?' It's instinctual and creates a cycle—an endless, vicious cycle of mistrust. A cycle that proves Trust itself is fundamentally flawed.

"Today, we will hear more testimonies of those victimized by Trust. People who believed and placed their faith in others, only to be left full of regret. Their testimonies will demonstrate how this vicious cycle of blame works. Sometimes it's turned inward, and we blame ourselves. Sometimes it's turned outward, and we look to blame someone else. But the result is always the same: mistrust grows, relationships crumble, and hope fades away.

"And as we will continue to prove, Trust isn't just flawed. It's dangerous. It's guilty."

Reed strides to the prosecution's table and pulls out a deck of Uno cards. Yes. Uno.

The jury looks at each other, shrugging their shoulders and pinching their brows together. Whispers trickle through the gallery. "What in the . . . ?"

Reed places the deck on the evidence table, fanning out the cards.

"Ladies and gentlemen of the jury," his voice dripping with smugness, "the prosecution introduces *Exhibit F: The Game of Uno*. Because nothing illustrates the blame game we play with Trust quite like this colorful and cutthroat deck of cards."

Pause for effect.

"Uno: The world's most passive-aggressive game." Reed holds the cards and starts flipping through them one by one. Reed explains,

- "Reverse: Blame the other person.
- "Draw Two: Escalate the conflict.
- "Wild Card: Blame your childhood traumas.
- "Draw Four? Congratulations, you've just blamed your ex, your boss, your parents, and global warming."

Laughter fills the courtroom. Even the bailiff cracks a smile.

Reed holds up a "Reverse" card. "The blame game, much like Uno, is all about strategy, avoidance, and self-preservation. When Trust breaks, what's our first instinct? We look for someone to blame. And just like this card, we're quick to "Reverse" the blame onto someone else."

He flips the card onto the jurors' box.

"But what happens when we can't find someone else to blame?" Reed pulls a yellow "Draw Two" card. "We turn inward, we escalate the conflict, forcing ourselves to 'draw' from a deck of guilt and shame. 'What did I do wrong? How could I have prevented this?'

Next, Reed dramatically holds up a "Wild Card." "And then, there's the Wild Card. Random, unpredictable, and impossible to prepare for. 'Why did they betray me? What was their real motive? Did I miss something?'"

Last, Reed flashes the "Draw Four" card to the jury. "This little guy is a game changer. You pull this card, and you've got plenty of blame to go around. You get a blame. You get a blame. On and on you go. Where you stop, nobody knows. The blame game is a cycle of chaos. Nobody truly wins, and everyone walks away angry and irritated."

Reed hesitates for a moment.

"And with that, Your Honor, the prosecution calls our next witness, Ms. Jordan Phillips. Ms. Phillips knows the blame game all too well."

A young adult, Jordan Phillips's jet black hair bounces as she strides in, wearing black heels. Her blue dress waves as everyone watches her walk to the witness stand. She fidgets nervously, subtly biting her lip as her eyes dart around the room. She settles into the witness chair, asks the bailiff for a glass of water, and takes a swig.

"Ms. Phillips, thank you for being here. Would you state your name and occupation for the court?"

She sips the water and clears her throat. "Jordan Phillips, and I'm a cosmetology student."

"Thank you. Now, would you please share with the court an experience from your childhood that shaped your ability to trust?"

"When I was eight, my dad promised he'd come to my basketball game. I'd been practicing for months, hours every day." Jordan sips her water like she's been wandering in the desert for hours. "I was so excited. I kept looking out into the audience, waiting to see him. But . . . he never showed up."

"And was this an isolated incident?"

"No." Jordan shakes her head, tightly gripping the glass. "Another time, he promised to take me camping. I packed my clothes. I even pulled out our tent from storage. But it never happened. Another time, he promised we'd build a treehouse together. I was so excited. I made a list of all the items we needed from the hardware store. I really got my hopes up. But of course, it didn't happen. After a while, I started wondering . . . was it me? Did I do something wrong? Was I not important enough? Did I not matter?" She reaches for a tissue and dabs the corner of her eyes.

"And how has that affected you today?"

"It's hard to trust anyone. I'm always waiting for the other shoe to drop, for people to let me down. If my dad couldn't come through for me, how could I possibly trust anyone else?"

Reed addresses the jury. "Ladies and gentlemen, this is the cycle of blame in action. Jordan's father repeatedly failed to keep his promises. It didn't just break her trust; it destroyed her sense of self-worth. You see, this is what Trust does. He leaves scars that never fully heal.

"Your Honor, at this time I'd like to introduce *Exhibit G* into evidence."

The bailiff swoops in and sets a tattered doll down on the evidence table. Its blue dress is a faded Carolina blue and torn, ripping at the seams. Its blonde pigtails are a frizzy, tangled mess of neglect. The chipped porcelain face displays a prominent crack down the middle, and the worn painted makeup that once depicted a smiling doll now looks like the meh emoji.

"This," the prosecutor parades the doll in front of the jury, "is *Exhibit G: A Broken Doll*, a symbol of shattered childhood trust, a once-cherished toy now tossed aside. Discarded, like trash. Not because it wasn't loved. It's because it wasn't protected. This broken doll represents the emotional wreckage caused by broken trust and the failure of those sworn to protect us."

WHAM! Reed slams the doll down on the table in disgust. Pieces of the once-cracked face explode everywhere. "Jordan is one of countless others. How can you possibly argue that Trust is reliable when its track record is devastating?"

Returning to his seat, Reed says, "No further questions."

Shield stands, buttoning his jacket. "Your Honor, permission to cross-examine?"

Judge Steele barely glances up. "Proceed."

"Jordan, Ms. Phillips, thank you. That couldn't have been easy. I have a young daughter myself and the thought of disappointing her or worse, breaking her heart, is tough to imagine."

Jordan slowly nods.

"Ms. Phillips, you mentioned your father missed your basketball game and other important events. Did he ever explain why?"

"He said he got busy." Jordan rolls her eyes.

"Was he busy with work, perhaps?"

"I guess," Jordan shrugs.

"Did he ever say something like, 'My boss made me work' or 'I had to work late'? Anything like that?"

"Yeah, he mentioned that a few times."

"Do you think it's possible that he was trying to provide for your family? Do you think he wanted to miss those moments?"

"Honestly, I don't know. The more it happened, the less I cared." Her lips curl before she takes another drink.

"Speaking from experience, there are times parents want to be there for their children but their job forces them to work extra hours, late nights, weekends even. I know that's not fair, but do you think that's his fault?"

"I suppose not. If he couldn't get off work and his boss made him work, what can he do?" Jordan shrugs, nodding. "When you're a child, those thoughts don't really cross your mind."

"Ms. Phillips, did you ever ask your father to take time off of work to spend time with you?"

"Yes, as a matter of fact, I did."

"And what happened?"

"He showed up. He spent time with me, and we had some great memories. But it doesn't extinguish the pain from before."

"I completely understand. Being a parent is hard. Having a career and providing for your family is difficult. Sometimes, it's a burden we wish we didn't have to carry. But let me ask you this: did your father show up for you more often than not?"

"Hmm," Ms. Phillips squints, looking toward the ceiling for a moment. "I would say so. He let me down a lot, but he also was there for me, too."

Shield turns to face the jury. "Ladies and gentlemen, Jordan's story is heartbreaking, no doubt about it. The job of a parent is one of the most difficult. It's sometimes impossible to have a work-life balance. Something always gives. But do you see what happened here? There are negative moments. Moments of hurt and anguish. But there are also positive ones. Moments of joy and fond, precious memories. The prosecution wants you to solely focus on the negative and completely ignore the positive. If we condemn Trust for all these negatives, we're completely obliterating any opportunity for the positives. Life is full of positives and negatives. We can't have one without the other. I hope you see that. Is the issue here Trust? Or is it us?"

He steps back, taking a moment to stare at the jury. His point lingering. Seed of doubt planted.

Reed gets up and returns to the evidence table, picking up the Uno deck again.

"Let's talk about the wild nature of trust," he says, shuffling the cards. "Trust operates like this deck. Sometimes it works in your favor, a 'Skip' card lets you avoid trouble. But more often than not, it's a 'Draw Four,' leaving you scrambling to recover.

"At the end of the day, this is a stacked deck. And just like a bad hand of Uno, Trust leaves us vulnerable to attack."

Reed introduces his next witness. "The prosecution calls Mr. Michael Evans."

A middle-aged man with three strands of hair carefully combed back rises from the gallery. The overhead lighting casts a shine on his head. His white short-sleeved shirt complete with pocket protector is half untucked and exploding at the seams, his belly threatening to launch one of the buttons like a missile into the gallery. His glasses fall just off the bridge of his nose. With each step toward the witness stand, a struggled wheeze escapes his lips. He swears the oath and settles in. He plops into the chair and leans back, tightening his jaw.

"Mr. Evans, would you mind telling the court about your experience with Trust in the workplace?"

"I worked for the same company for fifteen years. I gave them everything. Late nights. Weekends. Constant sacrifices," Michael growls. "I trusted them when they promised to reward my loyalty. And then one day out of the blue, they called me to the office and handed me a severance letter. No warning. No explanation. Just an uncomfortable discussion and a box to pack up my desk."

The jury murmurs. One juror leans slightly forward, crossing her arms. Another presses their lips together, their gaze flickering between Trust and the witness.

"Mr. Evans, that doesn't seem fair. Would you say the severance letter made you feel betrayed by your company, proving that trust is dangerous?"

The defense rises. "Objection, Your Honor, leading the witness."

The judge nods. "Sustained. Counsel, rephrase your question."

"Yes, Your Honor. I'll rephrase. Mr. Evans, how did that severance letter affect you?"

"I don't trust anyone anymore. Not my bosses, not my coworkers . . . not even myself."

"Thank you, Mr. Evans. Your Honor, at this time I'd like to enter into evidence *Exhibit H: A severance letter.*"

The bailiff sets a crisp piece of paper down on the evidence table. Picking it up, Reed presents it to the jury. Doing his best Vanna White impression.

Oooh. Ahhh.

"This is Exhibit H. A severance notice. A cold, impersonal document that represents the betrayal of trust in institutions. A breach of contract on the most personal level. Michael's story isn't an outlier; it's a reflection of a society that promises security and delivers disappointment."

Reed places the letter back on the table. "Your Honor, no further questions."

Shield rises, buttoning his jacket. (You know, these lawyers must spend a pretty penny on jacket buttons. Unbuttons jacket. Buttons jacket. Rinse, repeat, on a seemingly never-ending loop. I wonder how many suit buttons they go through in a given year. Do you think that's an unwritten line item in the attorney fees?)

"Mr. Evans, I'm sorry to hear your company laid you off. I've lost a job or two over the years. That must have been incredibly difficult. You said you worked for the same company for fifteen years. During that time, did you receive raises? Promotions? Recognition for your hard work?"

"Uhh . . . yes." His chest rises and falls, as his words come in fragments. Each word is a battle against his own breathlessness.

"And would you say that, for most of those fifteen years, your trust in the company was well-placed?"

"I guess so, but—"

"I understand. But isn't it fair to say that your experience wasn't defined by betrayal but by a moment of human or corporate failure?"

"It's possible. But if I would've known they would've hung me out to dry like that, I never would've stuck my neck out. I wouldn't have worked all those hours and sacrificed. They just took advantage of me and let me go like I was expendable."

"Mr. Evans, that's awful. Hindsight is always twenty-twenty. Unfortunately, we don't have the benefit of knowing how things will unfold before they happen. But let me ask you, do you think if you didn't work those late nights and long hours, they would've fired you sooner?"

"I'm not really sure. But based on how everything went, I'd say, yeah. I believe they would have."

"Mr. Evans, it sounds to me like your company took advantage of you. Do you think they used your desire for job security and career advancement against you?"

"100 percent. They used me until it no longer suited their needs."

"Mr. Evans, if your company used you and took advantage of you, then why are you here blaming Trust? Did you ever consider filing suit again your former employer for wrongful termination?"

"Well, no."

"Why not? It sounds to me like there's potential there."

"I didn't have the money for a lawyer. I didn't have time to wait around on the courts and hope to win a civil dispute."

"Mr. Evans, I understand. Thank you for your time."

Shield turns to the jury. "Ladies and gentlemen, did Trust fail Mr. Evans? Was it Trust that took advantage of Mr. Evans and manipulated him into working long hours and weekends? Or was it a flawed system run by imperfect people?"

Shield pauses before returning his seat.

Reed quickly calls his next witness, careful to interrupt the silence.

Ms. Mandy Payne, a woman in her early thirties, enters the courtroom. She's wearing a gray pants suit and a white ruffly shirt. Her large hoop earrings sway as she walks. As she approaches the stand, there's a noticeable twitch of her left pinky finger.

"Ms. Payne, would you tell the court about your experience with broken trust?"

"I was married for six years. I thought we were happy." She rubs her left pinky against a phantom wedding ring. "But then I found out the cheating bastard was fooling around on me for two of those years. And if that wasn't bad enough?" She crosses her arms and wrinkles her nose as her lips curl down. "It was with someone I considered a friend."

A collective wince ripples through the jury, like the pain when you stomp on a Lego with your bare feet.

"How did that affect you, Ms. Payne?"

"It . . . broke me. I wondered if it was my fault. Was I not enough? Could I have done something different? Something more? But then I realized . . . it wasn't me. It was him. He was the liar. He was the one who couldn't keep it in his pants."

One juror snorts. Someone in the back raises their hand, "Preach."

"Order! I'll have order in my court." Judge Steele slams the gavel.

Reed gestures to the judge. "Your Honor, I'd like to enter into evidence *Exhibit I: a torn wedding photo.*"

The bailiff places a torn photograph of the once-happy couple on the evidence table.

Trust shifts uncomfortably in his seat at the defense table. He drops his shoulders, purses his lips together, and looks down as he stares at the photo. His chin drops to his chest. How could the jury not feel for this woman? Trust certainly does.

"This," Reed exclaims, "is Exhibit I, a reminder of how infidelity shatters trust. Ms. Payne's story is one of countless others. Further proof that trust is not just fragile; it's dangerous, it's irredeemable."

Shield rises. "Objection, Your Honor, speculation."

The judge acknowledges. "Sustained. Counsel, stick to the facts."

"Apologies, Your Honor, withdrawn. Nothing further."

Shield calmly rises and approaches the witness. "Ms. Payne, I'm so sorry. I can't begin to imagine how difficult this must be. I'm incredibly sorry you had to go through such an ordeal. If I may, how did your ex-husband react when you told him you knew about the affair?"

"Oh, he lied. He tried to make me feel crazy. Like I was the one with the issue. Classic, right? But little did he know, I already had proof."

"I see. That's awful. People should take accountability for their actions rather than shifting the blame. Now, based on your prior testimony, you are divorced, correct?"

"Yes."

"And during the divorce, did you receive restitution? Alimony? Anything like that?"

"I absolutely did." She rubs her pinky across the phantom wedding ring. "I hired the best divorce attorney I could afford and I took him to the cleaners. I got half of everything."

"Ms. Payne, it sounds like you were able to hold him accountable for his actions, is that correct?"

"Yes and no. Even though I received some compensation, it doesn't change what happened. It doesn't remove the pain and hurt of what he did to me, to our family." She clenches her jaw, nostrils flaring a smidge. "As much as I hate to say it, I would rather be married than what the end result was."

"Ms. Payne, I'm truly sorry. That is heartbreaking. Thank you."

Shield turns to the jury. "Ladies and gentlemen, let's think for a moment. Ms. Payne shared with us a devastating testimony. Her ex-husband betrayed her in the worst way. It's so upsetting the divorce rate in this country. But who is ultimately to blame here? Is it Trust who had an affair? Was it Trust who lied and attempted to blame Ms. Payne? Was it Trust who went behind her back? Should we condemn Trust, or should we be condemning human imperfection?

"No further questions, Your Honor." Shield walks back to the defense table, giving a slight fist bump toward Earnest Trust.

Reed gets back on his feet to drive the day's final point home.

"Trust is a menace to society. It's reckless, callous. And what happens when Trust fails? Trust leaves behind debris that can't be cleaned with any amount of 'I'm sorry's.' No, ladies and gentlemen. Trust's failures leave life-long scars.

"Jordan. Michael. Mandy. They represent ALL of us. Their stories aren't anomalies. They're the rule, not the exception. We have all fallen victim to Trust's lies and deception. And now we have an important choice in front of us: do we let Trust off the hook, ready to ruin more lives? Or do we do what must be done?"

The courtroom is deathly silent.

The jury is a mix of emotions. Some sit with their arms crossed. Others stare at their hands, checking their manicures. One bites their lip like it's their favorite flavor of bubble gum.

And Trust? These last two days have taken quite a toll. His hair is a mess, sticking up in all the wrong places. His suit is littered with wrinkles as he sits for hours each day, shifting this way and that. Earnest Trust is battered, bruised. But he hasn't given up. There's plenty of fight left in him. And that's a problem for the prosecution. Because when they think they've won, the defense plants something sinister. A sliver of doubt. It's crucial to remember: conviction requires proof beyond a reasonable doubt.

The judge smashes the gavel. "Court is adjourned." The courtroom empties and the battle rages on. Day Two is in the books.

The defense consultation room is about the size of Harry Potter's cupboard underneath the stairs. It smells of stale coffee and old paper. The fluorescent lights buzz overhead.

Harvey Shield loosens his tie, giving himself a moment to breathe after the day's events. Trust and Shield sit across from each other, locked in an epic starring contest.

Shield loses, breaking the silence. "The prosecution offed us a deal." He slides the plea deal across the table. "Fifteen years. Eight with good behavior. No appeals. No circus. It'll pass by in no time. This will be over and done with and in your rearview."

Trust looks frozen, he doesn't move a muscle. Not so much as a blink.

Then, *BOOM.* "You want me to admit to something I didn't do?!" Trust erupts, slamming his fist on the table. "You think in fifteen years they'll see me any differently? In eight years, they'll somehow forget?

35

Accepting this deal is admitting guilt. That's not freedom. That's not justice. That's death by 5,475 paper-cuts."

"Look, this isn't about justice," Shield pinches the bridge of his nose. "It's about survival. Look at the jury. Look at their faces, Trust. Look at the headlines. The deeper this rabbit hole goes, the tougher it is to climb out. If you take this deal, you live to fight another day. Right now, the prosecution is making you look like a lying, cheating, two-faced backstabber."

Trust crosses his arms. "Then, we fight. I didn't come this far to give up now. There's still a chance to come out of this thing on top. I might bend, but I refuse to break. EVER!"

Shield stares at him like he's watching Mel Gibson's Freedom Speech from *Braveheart*. He heavily sighs, grabs the plea deal, and folds it in half. Then in half again. Then just once more to really annoy the bajeezus out of Reed.

"Understood." He stands, tucking the plea deal into his pocket, and heads for the door.

Before stepping out, Shield pauses. "Once I walk out that door, there's no going back."

Trust nods without hesitation. Game on.

Standing outside, Curtis Reed leans against the hallway. The arrogance that oozes from this guy is unreal. His smirk set to "Douchebag."

He doesn't even look up when Shield approaches.

Shield is all business. Without breaking stride, he pulls the tiny plea deal from his pocket and slaps it into Reed's hand.

"No deal."

Reed blinks, attempting to process what just happened.

Before Reed has a chance to respond, Shield is halfway down the hall, bounding toward the courthouse doors.

Reed glances down at the paper football-sized plea deal in his hand. His smirk evaporates, replaced with pure rage. He cracks his neck like a *Bond* villain and mutters under his breath, glaring in Shield's direction. "All right, Shield. Let the games continue."

The courthouse doors slam shut.

CHAPTER 3

Control is an Illusion

THE AIR INSIDE THE COURTROOM is heavier today. If Day One set the stage and Day Two fanned the flames, then Day Three throws a Molotov cocktail into the fray. Pleasantry and decorum are long gone, replaced by urgency from both sides. The courtroom's a pressure cooker about to blow.

The courthouse doors swing open at nearly the same time. Harvey Shield and Curtis Reed awkwardly and in unison step inside. The two legal titans lock eyes. There's a tremendous amount of bad blood between them. Reed is still fuming from Shield's stunt with the paper football plea bargain.

"You've got some nerve, Shield."

"Well, good morning to you, too, sunshine," Shield barely glances up from his notepad.

"I hand you a gift. A way out. And this is how you repay me? You slap it right back in my face? Stupid doesn't even begin to cover it." Reed's face grows redder by the second, squinting his beady little eyes. He's a few breaths away from a fire-breathing dragon or a heart attack.

Shield doesn't seem bothered. His calm aura is an exaggerated *yaaaaawn.*

"You done?"

"Oh, I'm far from done," Reed laughs, clenching his teeth together. "You've unleashed the beast. No more Mr. Nice Guy. I'm gonna tear you apart piece by piece, brick by brick. You've sealed your fate. Do you hear me? By the time this is all over, you'll be begging for mercy . . ."

Shield casually raises a hand and brushes an invisible speck of dust off his shoulder in a slow, mocking motion. "Good luck with that."

Reed stands there, clenching his fists, like a volcano ready to erupt.

Shield takes his seat, smirking to himself. He knows what he's doing. And so does Reed. Shield's engaged in mental terrorism, and Reed's playing right into it.

The gallery is dead silent as the jury shuffles in, whispering amongst themselves.

Earnest Trust sits up straight, holding his chin high. His defiance in the face of defeat seems to reinvigorate him. He looks surprisingly well-rested with just a hint of baggage under his eyes. He has a hardened expression. And if you stare long enough and ignore your parents' rule that it's not polite to stare, you'll notice a slight twitch at the corner of his lip. A renewed confidence radiates from the defendant, but how long will it last?

Reed launches out of his chair like a man possessed. "Ladies and gentlemen of the jury, today marks the conclusion of the prosecution's case against Trust.

"Over the past two days, we've shown you the undeniable truth. Trust is a fraud, a contract breaker, a repeat offender, fully complicit in his crimes. And today? Today, we will prove beyond a shadow of a doubt that Trust is a ticking time bomb.

"Trust lures us in with a false sense of security, seducing us into believing we're safe. But just when we let our guard down?

BAM!" Reed slams his hand on the jury box. "It pulls the rug right out from under us."

The jury shifts, some nodding, some frowning, some still sitting on the fence. And in the near distance, Earnest Trust clenches his hands, rocking back and forth in the defendant's chair as he leans in.

Reed lowers his voice. "Ladies and gentlemen, we are at a crossroads. You've heard the testimony. You've seen the broken contracts, the shattered lives, and the betrayals stacked a mile high. And today, we take it one step further. Today, we expose the grand illusion, the desperate grasp for control that follows every betrayal. Because that's what we do, isn't it? When Trust fails us, we struggle to regain control. We build walls. We cut people off. We convince ourselves that if we can hold the reins a little tighter, we'll never get hurt again.

"But here's the truth: control is an illusion, a false promise. And when it fails, it leaves us questioning everything—ourselves, our relationships, and even God himself."

Stopping, Reed lets the silence build.

"So I ask you, why should anyone, including God, be trusted if Trust is so fragile, unreliable, and dangerous?"

The prosecution calls its next witness, a middle-aged woman named Susan Sampson. She rises from the gallery and approaches the stand, clutching a tissue at her side. Her eyes are glassy and her posture resembles a deflated balloon. Her hair is like an October pumpkin patch. Her flowy polka dot dress waves at the gallery behind her while her clopping short white heels signal her arrival.

"Mrs. Sampson, can you tell the court why you're here today?"

"When my husband left, I promised myself I would never allow my kids to experience that kind of pain," she sniffles, wiping her nose with the tissue. "So I, I became . . . controlling, a dictator."

The courtroom shifts, wincing as she delivers her testimony.

"I monitored their every waking move. I had their locations pinned. Their texts were synced to my tablet. If they so much as sneezed in the direction of a bad decision, I knew about it. I thought I was protecting them," Susan sighs loudly, sniffling and dabbing her eyes, careful not to ruin her makeup.

"Ms. Sampson, how is your relationship with your children now?"

"We have a strained relationship. The older they got, the more they started to pull away. They stopped coming to me for advice. Now, I rarely talk with them anymore. They barely call me, and if they do, it's just because it's someone's birthday or a holiday." She lifts her head, trying to keep the tears in her eyes from falling out. She lets out a calming breath and continues, "When we get together for the holidays, the kids are constantly bringing up how I never let them do anything when they were younger, how I constantly controlled every aspect of their lives. I thought I was building up walls to keep them safe. But what I really did was isolate everyone, myself included. Now, I'm the one on the outside looking in."

"Ms. Sampson, would you say your desire, your need for control, came from a place of fear?"

"Yes. I couldn't trust anyone else—not their teachers, not their friends, definitely not their father." Tears stream down her face. She sniffs hard but it does little to stop the steady drip from her reddened nose. "When their father walked out on us, it broke our family. I swore I would never let anyone hurt them again."

"And would you say that fear destroyed the Trust you were trying to protect?"

"Yes." Susan clutches her tissue, her voice cracking. "I thought if I just controlled everything, they'd never get hurt. If I just never Trusted their father, then we wouldn't be in this situation. It was my fault for Trusting him. But even more, it was Trust's fault. It's because of Trust and his failures that I built up these walls. And in the end, it's because of Trust that I ended up hurting them most."

Trust lets out a slow, deep breath. His hands clench just a little bit tighter as he places them behind his head. His eyes drop to the table, struggling to make sense of it all. Another witness, another knife plunged into his back.

Turning to the jury, Reed gestures to a photograph of a towering, impenetrable wall.

"Ladies and gentlemen, this is *Exhibit J: The Wall of Isolation*. This represents the walls we build to protect ourselves when Trust fails. Susan's story is not unique; it's a universal reaction to broken Trust.

"We think these walls will shield us from pain, but they trap us in isolation. Trust drives connection. And when it fails, we hide. We isolate ourselves, destroy relationships, and in the end . . . no one wins. This is the inevitable result of Trust's failures."

"Objection, Your Honor," Shield leaps, knocking the chair backward. "Counsel is assuming facts not in evidence. Ms. Sampson's actions may have stemmed from fear, but they don't prove that Trust itself is to blame."

"Sustained. Counselor, reframe your argument," Judge Steele rules.

"Fair enough. Let's not blame Trust then." Reed taps the photo for emphasis. "But rather, his inherent fragility. This wall exists because Trust failed to hold under the pressure, and that is the point, Your Honor."

Shield rises, adjusting his jacket for the umpteenth time. "Ms. Sampson, thank you for your testimony. Your story is devastating and every parent's nightmare where their kids grow up, move away, and barely speak to each other. I can't imagine how hard it must have been raising your children alone."

"It wasn't easy," Susan sniffles, dabbing the tissue underneath her eyelids.

"You said your actions came from a place of love. I believe that they were. But would you say your intentions were good, even if the outcome wasn't what you hoped for?"

"Yes, I suppose so."

"Do you think if you could go back and do it all over again, you would try to control so much of your children's lives?"

"Um," Susan runs her fingers through her hair, taking a moment to contemplate. "I don't think that I would. I think I would've given them a longer leash, let them make their own choices, and just try to be there for them as best as I could."

"Ms. Sampson, I completely understand. I know it's a tough question, especially when we can't know what the future holds. But answer me this: if you did give your kids more leeway to make their own decisions, what kind of impact would that have had on your family?"

"Objection, Your Honor. Speculation," Reed stands from his chair, motioning towards Ms. Sampson. "Council is asking the witness to speculate."

"Your Honor, if you'll just indulge me for a moment, you'll see the reason. Ms. Sampson is innately qualified to speak about her life and her past."

"Hmm," Judge Steele looks back and forth between the counselors. "Overruled, but get to the point, Mr. Shield. The witness may answer."

"Thank you, Your Honor."

"I think it would've had a huge impact. Seeing the damage my attempts to control their lives inflicted, I think we all could've benefited greatly from more Trust. It was my fault for not Trusting my kids to do the right thing."

"Thank you, Ms. Sampson." Shield approaches the jury. "Ladies and gentlemen, Susan's story is heartbreaking. Our capacity to Trust breaks when we place our Trust in the wrong hands. When people betray us, when they break our Trust, it's only natural to isolate ourselves, to build up walls. But we cannot confuse our actions driven by fear with the failure of Trust itself."

He stops, looking at the jurors and around the courtroom.

"Ms. Sampson's struggle was not with Trust. It was with fear and loss. The pain caused by her ex-husband leaving created a spiral effect. It was her ex-husband that broke her Trust and caused her to isolate, to build up walls and shield her children. It wasn't Trust. And that's the real question here, isn't it? Is it fair to blame Trust when the real problem is the pain caused by personal betrayal?

"No further questions."

Trust seems to relax for the first time all day. His shoulders rest a little lower instead of squeezed tightly, inching closer to his neck. He wipes his sweaty palms along his pants and leans a little further back in his chair.

Meanwhile, Reed scribbles frantically in his notebook, probably something like, "*This *bleeeeeep.*"

"Your Honor, redirect?" Reed says to Judge Steele.

"Proceed."

"Ms. Sampson, you blamed Trust's failures for your walls of isolation. But just a moment ago, you said you think having more Trust toward your kids would've been the better option. But isn't it true that it's because you Trusted your ex-husband that all these control issues reared their ugly head?"

"Yes, that's true. If I never Trusted him and he never betrayed our family's trust and walked out, then I probably wouldn't even be here today."

"Thank you, Ms. Sampson. No further questions."

Reed seizes the opportunity to call his next witness. "Your Honor, the prosecution calls Dr. Hannibal Lecture."

The courtroom doors swing open and a sudden gust of cool air rushes into the room. Dr. Hannibal Lecture, a man in his mid-sixties, bursts through the void, wearing a three-piece black suit with a gray vest. It creates a nice contrast and accents his silver combed-back hair. He takes his index finger and presses his glasses back toward the bridge of his nose as he makes his way to the stand with a confident gait. He swears the oath and takes a seat, crossing one leg over the other. With a glance at the jury, he straightens his glasses.

"Dr. Lecture, thank you for being with us today. Can you please tell the court your occupation?"

"Certainly. I am a college professor at the University of Florida."

"And what are you a professor of, Dr. Lecture?"

"I am a professor of philosophy and multi-cultural studies." Dr. Lecture takes off his glasses, wipes them briskly with his handkerchief to remove a stray fingerprint, carefully inspects them, and then places them back on his face.

"Thank you, Dr. Lecture. Now, as a professor, do you teach on the topics of Trust and on good and evil?"

"As a matter of fact, I do." His lips curl upward as a grin emerges. "The problem with Trust is the problem of evil. If God is all-powerful, he could stop suffering, right? If he is all-good, he would want to, yes? And yet, suffering still exists. Pain is all around us. This contradiction undermines the very foundation of Trust."

Some jurors shift in their seats. A few fiddle with their pens. Others nod in agreement.

"Dr. Lecture, that's a great point. How would you view humanity's desire to Trust in a higher power?"

"How can anyone Trust a God who allows children to die, wars to rage, and disasters to destroy? Either he isn't trustworthy or he doesn't exist. Trust in God is irrational," Dr. Lecture says as his hands rest on top of his knee. "An all-powerful, all-good being cannot coexist with the amount of evil we see in the world."

Loud gasps echo in the courtroom.

"Objection, Your Honor," Shield shouts, knocking his chair back several feet. "The witness is offering an opinion rather than evidence. This is precisely what the prosecution wants to distract this court with. You can't put Trust on trial without addressing the biggest gamble of all: faith. Without Trust, you can't have faith. Because if Trust falls, what happens to belief?"

"Overruled." Judge Steele rubs his temple, responding in a monotone fashion. "Dr. Lecture is qualified as an expert witness and may present his philosophical conclusions."

Shield frowns and doodles in his yellow notepad.

Reed dramatically motions toward the evidence table where a busted old clock sits. Its hands are frozen in place.

"Ladies and gentlemen, this is *Exhibit K: The Broken Clock*, the perfect representation of what happens when Trust fails. It symbolizes our attempts to control time, outcomes, and circumstances when Trust fails. When Trust is gone, what do we do? We overcorrect. We over-analyze. We micromanage like the world's worst boss. We cling to control with every fiber of our being.

"But the real joke . . . control is an illusion. And when control fails, we end up right back where we started—stuck, frozen in time, trapped in the same cycle of mistrust and despair."

Reed pauses, taking a few steps back.

"Ladies and gentlemen, let's be honest. If we can't even Trust one another, how can we possibly Trust a God we can't see? How many times have people put their faith in him, only to feel abandoned? How many prayers go unanswered? How many tragedies happen every day? And that, ladies and gentlemen, is the ultimate betrayal. No further questions for the witness."

Trust shifts in his chair, resting his head on his hand. Trust starts nervously bouncing his right leg, causing the glass of water on the table to vibrate. His heavy, downturned eyelids focus on the jury. As he adjusts his tie, there's a noticeable tremor in his hands. Trust looks more fragile, more human than ever.

A smirk crosses Reed's face as he observes Trust's unsteady manner. This plays right into his hands.

Shield approaches the witness stand. "Dr. Lecture, you've presented some compelling arguments today. But before we address that, I want to be very clear about something. God is not on trial here today. Trust is. Why did you decide to mention God in your testimony today?"

"It's quite simple, isn't it?" Dr. Lecture lets a hot blast of air run from between his teeth. "Trust and faith are connected. Trust and God are connected. You can't have one without the other. I've been listening to some of the testimony here today, and it is a common thread. Trust, faith, faith, Trust."

"I see. Now, Dr. Lecture, let's talk about free will. I assume you're familiar with free will, yes?"

"Free will explains human evil, perhaps," Dr. Lecture smirks, running his fingers down his smile lines. "But it does not explain natural disasters or childhood illnesses."

"That's true. I agree with you. But let's take it one step further. Is it possible that God allows things to serve a greater purpose, one we might not fully understand?"

"That's quite convenient, don't you think?" Dr. Lecture crosses his arms and leans backward in his chair. "An appeal to mystery."

"Or maybe it's an acknowledgment that we don't have all the answers, that our perspective is limited in the grand scheme of things. Dr. Lecture, you stated that Trust in God is irrational. I take it you don't believe in a higher power?"

"I certainly do not." He folds his hands on his knees, tapping his index fingers on the opposite hands. "Trust, faith in a higher power is a coping mechanism. It helps people explain away things. It helps them rationalize. No, I Trust in what I can see, feel, taste, and touch."

"Dr. Lecture, if that's the case, how can we Trust you? Doesn't your lack of Trust introduce an unfair bias to this jury?"

"No, I don't believe it does. People should be able to rationalize and come to their own conclusions based on my extensive experience."

"So we should just Trust what you say because it's the rational thing to do? But what if you're wrong? What if our senses limit our capacity to realize the bigger picture? Dr. Lecture, if you were wrong, wouldn't you want to know?"

"Objection, Your Honor," Reed interrupts the line of questioning. "Council is badgering the witness."

"Sustained. Watch yourself, Counselor." Judge Steele points at Shield with his pen.

"Apologies, Your Honor. Withdrawn."

The jury takes notes, whispering to each other while they process Shield's argument.

Shield addresses the jury. "Dr. Lecture assumes that because our understanding is incomplete, the complete picture doesn't exist. He will tell you the answer is plain as day. I wonder how frequently we've labeled something as unfair, unnecessary, or even cruel, only to find it ultimately led to something meaningful? Important?

"Look, I get it. The idea of Trust, especially Trusting in something greater, isn't easy." It's messy. It's complicated. It's frustrating. But our lack of understanding doesn't mean there isn't a purpose. And blaming Trust is a copout. Maybe the biggest mistake we'll ever make."

"No further questions, Your Honor," Shield steps back, placing his hands in his pockets.

Reed pushes himself back and stands. "The prosecution calls Mr. Robert Jones to the stand."

Robert Jones, a man in his late forties, slowly rises from the gallery. He's wearing a red quarter-zip sweater and black slacks and clutching a photograph tightly to his chest with both arms. His shoulders slump forward and he looks down along the path to the witness stand, strands of his dark hair falling forward across his forehead.

Robert Jones steps into the witness stand and swears the oath. His hands are trembling even more than his voice as he utters, "I do."

"Mr. Jones, thank you so much for taking time out of your day to be here today. Can you tell the court why you're here?"

"About a year ago, my daughter was diagnosed with leukemia. She was seven years old." Mr. Jones looks down at the picture in his arms, tears welling up in his eyes. "We prayed every night. The church prayed. Everyone prayed. We Trusted that God would heal her."

"Take your time, Mr. Jones. I know this is difficult. What happened to your daughter?"

"She died anyway." Mr. Jones' shoulders tremble as he lets out a ragged breath. Tears streak down his flushed cheeks. He wipes at his face with the arm of his sweater. "It didn't matter. There's nothing we could do."

Silence. Tears and loud sniffles fill up the courtroom. Judge Steele hands Mr. Jones a box of tissues.

"I just don't understand. She was only seven. Why wouldn't God save her? She was innocent. How can I Trust him after this?"

Reed solemnly walks toward the evidence table, lifts a worn book high in the courtroom, and walks it in front of the jury.

"Ladies and gentlemen, this is *Exhibit L: The Prayer Journal.*" He flips through the pages, carefully pausing after each flip of the page. "Every page, every word is a cry for help, an expression of hope. Every word is proof of Trust, of faith. And page after page after page, the silence is deafening. No answer. This journal is evidence of Trust's failures, evidence of its heartbreaking crimes, evidence of God who stays silent."

Jurors look away, tears streaming down their faces. Some pinch the corners of their eyes, trying to subdue the flow. Reed doesn't speak, allowing everyone to contemplate the significance.

"Objection, Your Honor!" Shield exclaims. "The prosecution is speculating about God's intentions."

"Sustained," Judge Steele rules. "Prosecution, limit your argument to what can be reasonably inferred."

"Very well, Your Honor. Let me rephrase," tapping the journal. "While we cannot claim to know God's intentions, we can examine the impact of his silence. And that impact is devastating. No further questions."

The gravity of the moment isn't lost on Earnest Trust. He runs both hands down his face, leaving red finger streaks behind. His eyes are glassy, hearing the agony of Mr. Jones's testimony.

Shield empathetically approaches the witness stand.

"Mr. Jones, I'm so sorry for your loss. No parent should ever have to endure what you've been through. It's truly heartbreaking. I have a daughter of my own and the thought of losing her is absolutely devastating."

Robert nods, gripping the photograph and lingering on it for a few seconds.

"Mr. Jones, you mentioned that you prayed every day for your daughter's healing. And unfortunately, she passed away."

"Yes. We prayed. Every night, in fact. We believed. It didn't make a bit of difference."

"Mr. Jones, would you say that losing your daughter caused you to lose Trust in God?"

"Yes. How can I trust him after that?" Robert gulps, his lips quivering as he tries to hold back tears.

Shield turns slightly, gesturing toward the prayer journal on the evidence table. "I understand. But let me ask you this. During that time, did you feel supported by your family? By your church?"

"Yes," Robert hesitates. "But it didn't change anything. She's still gone. It didn't bring her back."

"Of course not. I'm sorry, Mr. Jones. I know this is tough. If I may, was your daughter in pain while she was dealing with her diagnosis?"

"All the time. She used to be so happy, so vibrant, always playing outside. I remember how she used to pick flowers from the front yard and tuck them behind my ear when she came inside." Tears are flowing in steady streams as Mr. Jones does his best to dab them with the tissue. "But the cancer wrecked her body. She barely left her bedroom. She could barely find the strength to eat."

"Mr. Jones, this is so heartbreaking. I can't imagine. Seeing a loved one in pain and suffering is so incredibly difficult. Mr. Jones, I know you said you have difficulty Trusting in God. But do you still believe in God?"

"I, um—I don't know. I guess so. I'm struggling to Trust him after he let my daughter die."

"I understand, Mr. Jones. Let me ask you this: do you believe in heaven?"

Reed leaps, knocking into the table and sending it a few inches off the ground. "Objection, Your Honor! Relevance?"

"Overruled. Sit down, Counselor. I want to hear this," Judge Steele sternly scolds Reed like he's getting put in timeout. "The witness may answer."

"Yes, I do believe in heaven. A few short weeks after she passed, I had a dream of my daughter. She was filled with joy. She was holding someone's hand and picking flowers with the brightest smile on her face. She looked so peaceful, glowing almost. I'd never seen her so happy. I woke with tears streaming down my face, but not tears of sadness. They were tears of joy. It reminded me that she's up there right now, watching over us, and she's not suffering anymore. She's cancer-free."

"Thank you, Mr. Jones. That seems comforting. You previously stated that your Trust in God was shaken. But did that dream, that encounter with your daughter in heaven shift your perspective?"

"Yes, it does. In fact, I'd like to change my answer from before. You asked if I still believe in God. I didn't seem sure. But, I can confidently say I do. I believe, and I believe that it was God's hand that my daughter was holding as she picked the most beautiful yellow and orange wildflowers from the field. I could sense deep down in my soul that everything was going to be all right. I just need to focus on the fact that she's no longer suffering but resting in the arms of God."

"Thank you, Mr. Jones." Shield faces the jury. "Ladies and gentlemen, Mr. Jones's pain is real. It's undeniable. His questions are valid. Losing a child is devastating. While Trust is on trial today, we must acknowledge that Trust and faith are connected. They're intertwined. One cannot exist without the other. Now, is it possible that God shows up in ways we don't always recognize or even understand? Does unanswered prayer mean that God has abandoned us?

Shield places his hands in his pockets as he walks down the line of the juror box. "If God's plans are bigger than our understanding, shouldn't we at least consider the possibility that his trustworthiness is greater than what we can see? Mr. Jones believes his daughter is in heaven, that she is no longer suffering. He Trusts that. He believes it. Even though he has questions, he continues to Trust. Isn't that our challenge today? When difficult circumstances come our way, will we condemn Trust or will we choose to point our Trust in the right direction? No further questions."

As Shield walks back to his seat, Trust sits a little taller and takes a slow, calming breath to settle himself.

Reed pushes his seat back and stands. "Your Honor, the prosecution calls its final witness: Mr. Gregory Nash, self-proclaimed atheist, author, and skeptic."

A quiet commotion fills the gallery. Gregory Nash, a man in his fifties, is a well-known author and speaker, notorious for his public denouncement of faith, Trust, and religion.

Gregory Nash rushes through the courtroom doors, wearing a black suit and button-down white shirt. His face is freshly shaven and his hair doesn't move as he struts to the witness stand. Gregory Nash affirms the oath, takes his seat, and folds his hands in front of him.

"Mr. Nash, thank you for taking time out of your busy schedule to be here today. Mr. Nash, what do you do for a living?"

"Well, I'm an author and a public speaker," he says, smiling widely.

"And how many books would you say you've sold?"

"Not to brag, but—" Mr. Nash pulls his suit jacket forward, flashing all his pearly whites, "several million."

"Mr. Nash, that's quite an accomplishment. Now, can you please tell the court your viewpoint regarding Trust?"

"Hah! Trust is humanity's greatest weakness," Nash smirks. "It's a flimsy concept we use to justify irrational beliefs and dangerous dependencies. I don't Trust people, institutions, or any gods because history has proven them unreliable," Nash says, shaking his head back and forth.

"Can you provide us an example of how Trust has led to harm?"

"Of course. Let's take religion."

GASP! The ultimate no-no. A foolproof plan to alienate yourself and everyone around you at the dinner table.

"Millions of people place their Trust in a divine being who supposedly loves them, who supposedly cares for them. And yet, they suffer. They die. Their prayers go unanswered. Wars have been fought, lives have been destroyed, entire cultures have been eradicated—all in the name of some higher power."

"And how does that align with the charges against Trust in this courtroom?"

Nash pauses, strumming his index finger on his chin like he's been waiting for this question all day. "Well, it aligns perfectly. Trust is the world's oldest con artist. He promises security, hope, and answers. But what he really delivers is heartbreak and disappointment. And you know the irony of it all? People keep falling for it—over, and over, and over again."

"Mr. Nash, is that the reason you label yourself as an atheist?"

"Absolutely. You don't see atheists and agnostics attempting to conquer the world and lay waste to entire civilizations in the name of atheism. The same can't be said about other religions. No, I don't trust in what I can't see. And what my eyes tell me and, further, what history has continually shown is that Trust is a fool's errand."

"Thank you, Mr. Nash. No further questions."

Trust cups his right hand and places it over his forehead. A poor attempt to hide himself from the damning testimony. A loud gush of wind escapes from his mouth. You can almost hear Trust whisper, "What. A. Jerk. This guy's just mean."

Shield rises, and yes . . . he adjusts his jacket. And he approaches the witness stand. "Mr. Nash, you've made it abundantly clear that you don't Trust anyone or anything. Is that correct?"

"Absolutely right," Nash leans back, chuckling as he folds his arms across his chest.

"Interesting. And yet, you're leaning back, Trusting that chair you're sitting in not to break under your weight. You Trust the jury to consider and believe your testimony. You Trust in your own reasoning, logic, and intellect. You've made dozens of Trust-based decisions from the moment you walked from your car until delivering your testimony here today. Isn't that right?"

"That's not the same Trust we're talking about."

"Isn't it though?" Shield raises an eyebrow. "Isn't it true that Trust isn't inherently the problem? It's where we place it, wouldn't you agree?"

Nash glares. (If looks could kill . . .) "I suppose you could argue that."

"And what about love, Mr. Nash? Do you believe in love?"

"Objection, Your Honor," Reed bounds from his leather seat. "Relevance?"

"Your Honor, if the court will give me a moment, you'll see the relevance."

Judge Steele squints at Shield. "Overruled, but get to the point. The witness may answer."

"Love? Love is complicated," Nash hesitates.

"It certainly is," Shield grins. "But isn't love a form of Trust? To love someone is to Trust them with your heart, your vulnerabilities, your very being. Are you saying love is a weakness, too?"

"I'm saying it's a risk," Nash pushes out air from between his teeth. "One that often leads to pain."

A satisfied Shield turns to the jury. "Ladies and gentlemen, that's precisely the point. The prosecution wants you to believe Trust is too dangerous because it involves risk. But risk is essential for everything worth having: love, hope, faith. Without Trust, we don't avoid pain. We lock ourselves away from joy, from connection, from purpose. The walls we build are so tall, we can't see the forest through the trees."

Shield turns back to Nash. "Tell me, Mr. Nash. If Trust is so foolish, so risky, then why should we trust you? No further questions, Your Honor."

With the prosecution's case coming to a close, Reed makes his final move. The bailiff lugs in a large, unoccupied chair and places it in the middle of the courtroom. Reed gestures toward the chair. "This is *Exhibit M: The Empty Chair.*"

Pause for effect.

"This is the prosecution's final piece of evidence." Reed steps behind the chair, tapping the back of it like he's playing the piano. "This chair symbolizes every moment where Trust has left us stranded. Like Tom Hanks on an island, screaming for WILSON! This is the seat of silence, the seat of abandonment, the seat of shattered faith."

Reed strides toward the jury, pacing slowly. "Ladies and gentlemen, throughout the course of this trial, we have exposed Trust for what it truly is. It is a fraud, a pretender, a con artist, an illusion."

Reed turns, pointing directly at Trust. "We do not argue that Trust is useless. We argue Trust is unreliable, a gamble no sane person should take. You've heard the testimonies. You've seen the evidence. Trust has failed us in every way imaginable: in love, in friendship, in connection, in business, in family, in leadership. And worst of all? It has failed us in faith."

The gallery whispers. The jury hasn't moved in some time, hanging onto Reed's words.

"So, I leave you with this. If even the most basic applications of Trust are unreliable, then why should Trust have a place at all within our lives?" Reed pauses, then swaggers back to his table. "The prosecution rests."

Judge Steele breaks the silence with a single crack of his gavel. "The prosecution has rested its case. The defense will present their case starting at 9 a.m. tomorrow morning. The jury will remember their admonition. Court is adjourned."

The jury stands. Some have their brows pinched. Others have their lips pressed together. A few of them pull at their shirt sleeves as they glance sideways and make their exit from the jury box. Loud commotion overtakes the gallery. Some are nodding in agreement in response to Reed's fiery plea. Others shake their heads in disgust, waving their hands violently, trying to get their point across. Reed has certainly done his part to stir the pot in an epic fashion. The totality of his case has left a lasting impact.

At the defense table, Earnest Trust sits still. A little too still. His shoulders hunch forward and he slinks down in his chair. His hands clench and unclench as he shakes his head back and forth. Rinse, repeat. Trust looks over at Shield with big puppy dog eyes. Is it a glimmer of hope? A look of desperation?

Harvey Shield acknowledges him. He sees it, feels it. He walks over and pats Trust on the shoulder, wraps an arm around him, and pulls him close. He whispers to him while nodding his head. You can almost make out the words, "hang in there" through the noise. He knows the real fight has just begun. This trial isn't over by a long shot.

The prosecution has thrown everything and the kitchen sink at Trust. And now, it's the defense's turn to strike back.

CHAPTER 4

The Defense Strikes Back

THE MAN WHO THRIVES on little sleep, copious amounts of coffee, and uncertainty steps into the courtroom. Harvey Shield survived three grueling
days of Reed's legal gymnastics, dodging cheap shots and body blows, but
today? Today, he goes on the offensive. Today, the defense strikes back.

Reed spent three long days smashing Trust's reputation with a metaphorical hammer, bludgeoning him to death. His arguments were conniv-
ing, ruthless. He handpicked his witnesses with heartbreak and grief in
mind. The jury soaked up every accusation, every testimony, every piece of
evidence like a sponge. And now, it's up to Shield to flip the script.

The bell rings. *Ding, Ding.* It's game time.

Trust sits, looking like a man who just got off a rollercoaster and is
about to hurl, but there's no trashcan in sight. His once sharp suit is now
crumpled like last week's newspaper. But behind the exhaustion and wors-
ening bags, Shield sees something else: a fire still burning.

"You ready?" Shield leans over.

"Ready," Trust slightly tips his head down. "Let's give 'em a show."

The gallery is on caffeine overload. There's more commotion and side
conversations happening today than in days past.

Judge Steele storms in with a fury, robe flowing behind him. He slams
the gavel down and immediately stops the ruckus.

"Counselor, is the defense ready to present their case?"

Shield rises and buttons his jacket. This is it. "We are, Your Honor."

He moves to the jury box. His gaze sweeps across the jury, the judge,
and the arrogant prosecutor.

"Ladies and gentlemen of the jury, we've spent several days listening to the prosecution's case. We've heard their witnesses. We've seen their exhibits. They've labeled Trust as a fraud, a co-conspirator, a villain. And let's be honest, Reed gave us one heck of a performance, didn't he? But today, the show is over, folks.

"For three days, you've been told Trust is a liar, a con artist, and a deceiver. That Trust is a criminal, engaging in deception, false promises, and disappointment. But they've pulled the wool over your eyes. Their hope is to manipulate you and distract you from the truth. Trust is not a criminal. He's not a co-conspirator. Trust is the victim! Deliberately framed, manipulated, and twisted beyond recognition. The issue isn't Trust; it's where we place it."

Shield pauses, letting his words sink in. The jury leans forward, hands clasped together.

"Think about your own lives—your relationships, your hopes, your dreams, your future. Think about the times you forgave when it hurt the most. Think about the moments of love, progress, and hope. What do they all have in common? They're built on Trust.

"Without Trust, there is no love, no hope, no growth, no second chances, no relationships, no connection, no nothing. Trust isn't the enemy. It's the glue holding it all together. And throughout the course of the trial, we will emphatically prove just that."

Pause for effect.

"The prosecution spent days picking Trust apart, but we're going to set the record straight. One of the oldest, most historically validated records of humanity's struggle with Trust is the Bible."

Reed squirms in his chair, pressing his thumb and index finger against his pursed lips.

"The Bible isn't just some old religious text. It's a historically accurate document. Archaeological finds, including the Dead Sea Scrolls, confirm its accuracy. The Bible contains numerous instances of broken Trust and redemption. And through its pages, we unlock the answers to the very questions at the center of this trial:

- *Why do bad things happen?*
- Why is there so much evil in the world?
- How can God *be trusted when the world feels so broken?*

"We will not ignore these questions. We will tackle them head-on."

A change sweeps through the courtroom. The jury is sitting up straight as an arrow. They haven't so much as blinked. They intently focus their attention on Trust. He's not some ghost sitting at the defense table. He's a real person, a wounded warrior. The cracks in his suit tell a story of survival, not weakness.

Trust leans forward, meeting their gaze, watching the jury as they analyze him. He's not broken, not defeated. He's anxious to prove the haters wrong.

Shield locks eyes with each juror. "Ladies and gentlemen, the prosecution has argued that Trust is unreliable, fragile, even dangerous. What the prosecution purposely left out of their argument is that Trust isn't the cause of his own failure. Trust didn't break himself. He was broken. The first betrayal of Trust wasn't in the Garden of Eden. It wasn't in a courtroom. It happened in heaven. That's right, Trust was first broken by none other than the devil himself."

A wave of discomfort sweeps through the courtroom. Reed tenses up, drawing his shoulders toward his ears.

"The prosecution asked, 'Why does evil exist if God is so good?' But let me ask this a different way. If evil exists, and I think we can all agree it does, then doesn't it follow that there is an author of that evil?

"You know the famous saying? '*The greatest trick the devil ever pulled was convincing the world he doesn't exist*'? Well, let me remind you he has been running another scam: convincing you that Trust is the problem, when in reality . . . Trust was his first victim.

"Lucifer wasn't always the devil. He was an angel of light. But he wanted more and overstepped his bounds, going so far as to stage a mutiny!"

Shield turns toward the evidence screen behind him. Isaiah 14:12–14 flashes in big, bold letters.

- "I will ascend into heaven."
- "I will exalt my throne above the stars of God."
- "I will sit on the mount of the congregation."
- "I will ascend above the heights of the clouds."
- "I will be like the Most High."

"These are five bold 'I wills,' five acts of treason. The devil broke Trust before we ever had a chance. He whispered the first lie. He planted the first seed of doubt. And now, he's convinced the world that Trust is the real villain. He's manipulated us into believing that Trusting in God is a fool's errand. That when Trust fails, it's because Trust was never worth having. But what if that's a lie? What if Trust was never the problem? What if misplaced Trust is the real issue here?

"The prosecution wants you convinced that broken Trust is evidence against God, that suffering, betrayal, and injustice are all proof that Trust is a lie. But let's follow the evidence, shall we?

- Broken marriages? Seeds of mistrust between spouses fester and grow into distance, doubt, and devastation.

- Corrupt institutions? Deception wrapped in authority, betrayal masked as leadership, leaving those who depend on them abandoned.

- Lies whispered into our hearts? Whispers that *'You're not enough. No one cares. God has abandoned you.'* This is the kind of poison that isolates, weakens, and destroys us from within.

"These aren't random coincidences. This is a carefully designed strategy. The prosecution wants you to condemn Trust, but shouldn't we be looking at the real culprit? Maybe the problem isn't that Trust is irredeemable. Maybe it's the devil who has corrupted it beyond recognition."

Shield stops in front of the jury box. "The prosecution has asked, 'If God is good, why does he allow suffering?' But if suffering exists, why is the first question focused on God's goodness? Shouldn't we recognize the influence of an enemy hell-bent on destruction? The fact that pain exists doesn't disprove God. It proves the devil's existence.

"God is not the author of evil. He's the answer to it. But the devil is clever. He's spent a lifetime running the same tired con, convincing humanity to blame God for the very pain he's caused. It's the perfect misdirection."

Shield looks around the jury, urging them in silence. "Let's go back to the first recorded moment of broken Trust in human history. The serpent didn't sneak up on Eve and declare, *'God is a liar!'* Oh no. He's far more crafty than that. Instead, he asked one simple question, *'Did God really say . . . ?'* (Genesis 3:1) These four simple words introduced doubt, stage left. A tiny crack formed in the foundation of Trust. Fast forward to today, and the devil's tactics haven't changed.

- *'If God loved you,* he wouldn't let you suffer.'

- *'If God were real, he'd answer your prayers immediately.'*

• 'If God was trustwor*thy, the world wouldn't be so broken.'*

"Lies. Every single one. This is not evidence against God but evidence of an enemy at work, an enemy desperate to destroy Trust at its core."

Shield inches closer. "Let me ask you: who benefits if you've been hurt, betrayed, or abandoned? Is it God? Who wants to heal and restore you? Or is it the enemy who feeds off your doubt? The real question isn't whether Trust is guilty. The question is whether you've been tricked into believing it is."

The question lingers in the air. Trust stares at the jury. His eyes squint, focusing on the jury pool, silently pleading, screaming even: "*See me for what I am. Not for how I've been misused.*"

Shield walks to the defense table and lifts a worn leather-bound book for the jury. "Your Honor, the defense moves to enter into evidence *Exhibit 1: The Bible.* This is a historically factual record of humanity's relationship with Trust."

The gallery shifts in their seats. A monsoon of whispers springs forth from the gallery. People turn on either side of themselves, clearing their ear holes, making sure they heard Shield right.

"Order! Order!" Judge Steele breaks through the turmoil with an epic gavel slam. He strikes it so hard it rises off the bench, almost levitating.

"This document has been preserved for thousands of years. Archaeological evidence such as the Dead Sea Scrolls confirm its authenticity and reliability. It has outlasted empires, endured wars, and witnessed the rise and fall of civilizations. And yet, the prosecution would have you believe that Trust is fragile, that it crumbles under the weight of time. This book says otherwise."

BOOM.

Before anyone can catch their breath, Reed launches out of his chair like he's been shot out of a cannon. "Objection! The Bible is a religious text! Not a legal document. Not a historical record. Introducing this as evidence would clearly bias the jury."

"Response, Counselor?" Judge Steele raises an eyebrow

"Your Honor, I find it curious that the prosecution wants to suppress the Bible when they've been using it to frame their arguments since day one." Shield smirks, gently shaking the Bible in Reed's direction. "The Garden of Eden, Judas's betrayal, the Greek word for 'believe'—where do you think they got that from?

"Why should the prosecution be allowed to use the Bible to attack my client, while we are prohibited from using it to support his defense? That's a blatant double standard."

Judge Steele pauses, tapping his cheek with his finger. "Overruled. Mr. Reed, you opened this door. Don't be upset at what comes out the other side. The Bible is admitted as Exhibit 1."

Score one for the defense.

Shield turns to the jury. "Ladies and gentlemen, the prosecution claims that Trust is a lost cause. But let's examine the story in Genesis more closely: the story of Adam and Eve. Mr. Reed painted this story as proof of Trust's failure, that Trust collapsed the second Eve took a bite of that forbidden fruit. But what he didn't tell you was the whole story."

Shield stops. The silence lingers. "Trust didn't fail. Humanity did. Before the fall, Adam and Eve walked with God. There was no suffering, no betrayal, no death. Trust wasn't broken. It was whole. So what changed? Did God suddenly become untrustworthy? Did he change his promises? Did he deceive them?

"No. Humanity disobeyed. They had a choice, and they chose wrong. They trusted themselves over God. And what was the result? Pain, suffering, a world unraveling at the seams. The prosecution would have you believe this is evidence against God. I would submit to you: its evidence against us. It is evidence of humanity's rebellion and the consequences of sin."

Shield leans in like he's sharing a secret with an old friend. "Let me ask you: if a builder designs a perfect bridge, one that can withstand any natural disaster, and someone sabotages it, do you blame the builder? Of course not. You blame the saboteur. God designed Trust to be strong. We are the ones who sabotaged it."

Shield emphatically points in Reed's direction, his jacket whistling at the abrupt movement. "The prosecution wants you to condemn Trust as hopeless, ruined, that Trust cannot be relied on. But if that were true, then why are we here? Why does Reed Trust the justice system? Why do you Trust this court to deliver a fair verdict? Why do we Trust in anything for that matter if Trust is as useless as they claim?"

Shield crosses his arms, letting the anticipation bubble. "It's because Trust isn't broken. It's just been placed in the wrong hands." Shield places the Bible on the evidence table and lets out a slow, controlled breath. It's time to dismantle the prosecution's biggest argument.

"The prosecution hit you with a loaded question. 'If God is so good, why does he allow suffering?' It's a great question, a heavy one. These aren't easy questions, and I won't insult your intelligence by serving up cheap, cookie-cutter responses. But I will offer a different perspective: God cares more about your understanding of sin and its consequences than alleviating those consequences in the short term. Suffering exists because sin exists. And where did that sin come from? Not from God. Not from Trust. But from humanity's decision to break Trust in the first place.

"You see, when Adam and Eve chose disobedience, they didn't just make a bad call. They opened the floodgates to pain, death, and brokenness. The world we see today is proof of what happens when we stop trusting God."

Shield pauses, letting the gravity of his words settle. "The prosecution wants to convince you that Trust is the problem, and not just any old problem but a criminal. But what if that's the biggest lie of all? What if Trust isn't the villain? What if Trust is the answer?"

Shield glances at Trust. The defendant is sitting a little taller. And the jury? Still wrestling. It's a mixture of agreeing nods and unconvinced frowns in the jury box. But maybe they're starting to see a different picture.

Shield adjusts his tie back and forth, trying to find the perfect balance. "Your Honor, the defense calls their first witness: Dr. Gideon Abrams."

Dr. Gideon Abrams pushes through the courtroom doors, wearing a light denim button-down shirt with the sleeves slightly rolled above the wrists and dark blue jeans. He's an elderly gentleman in his late sixties with a full head of gray hair. For an older fellow, his hairline is pristine. He's wearing tan hiking books with sand permanently fused to the soles. He leaves a sandy trail as he approaches. Opening the swinging door and entering the witness stand, he adjusts his glasses before swearing the oath.

"Dr. Abrams, thank you for being here today. Would you please state your name and occupation for the court?"

"Of course. Dr. Gideon Abrams, and I'm an archaeologist and historian of Middle Eastern culture. Glad to be here."

"Thank you, Dr. Abrams. And how long have you worked in that field?"

"Well, not to give away my age, but about forty years. It's been my life's work to uncover the mysteries and histories of the Middle Eastern world." Dr. Abrams pushes his glasses onto the bridge of his nose.

"Dr. Abrams, as an expert in archaeology and Middle Eastern history, can you please tell the court what we know about the moment God first spoke to Abraham?"

"We know this: the Lord told Abraham, 'Go from your country, your people, and your father's household to the land I will show you. I will make you into a great nation, and I will bless you; I will make your name great, and you will be a blessing' *(Genesis 12:1-2)*.

"Imagine this: you wake up one morning, God tells you to pack your bags. There's no cars, no GPS, no MapQuest. Just a promise: leave everything you know—your home, your family, your security—and walk until I tell you to stop."

"Dr. Abrams, from a historical perspective, how would a command like this have been received?"

"Hah! Unheard of," Dr. Abrams shakes his head, laughing. "Insanity. In the ancient world, your land, your family were everything. Leaving them behind? That wasn't just inconvenient, it was suicide. But Abraham didn't hesitate. He trusted. He stepped out in faith before he saw the full picture. He had faith in God's promise before he had any proof."

"And does history confirm the fulfillment of this promise?"

"Absolutely," Dr. Abrams smiles, crossing his arms and leaning backward in his chair. "Abraham traveled through Canaan, which was a foreign land to him, which was later given to his descendants. Abraham and his wife, Sarah, were old. Far too old in fact. Look at me. I know I'm on the younger side, but do I look like I could have kids at my age? Well, neither could they. At least that is what science would say. They were well past their childbearing years, and somehow they conceived. And Isaac was born. Through Isaac, Abraham's lineage became the great nation we now recognize today, exactly as God had promised."

Shield rubs his chin. "And was there a moment when Abraham was asked to do the unthinkable, wasn't there?"

"Yes, that's right." Dr. Abrams takes off his glasses, pointing them toward the jury as if he's giving an interview. "The Lord told Abraham, 'Take your son, your only son, Isaac, whom you love, and go to the region of Moriah. Sacrifice him there as a burnt offering on a mountain I will show you.' *(Genesis 22:2)*"

Cricket . . . Cricket. The air is sucked out of the room. Everyone in the courtroom sits on the edge of their seats, perfect posture and all.

"Dr. Abrams, as a historian, what do we know about this region of Moriah?"

"The region of Moriah is where the Temple Mount in Jerusalem stands today. It is one of the holiest sites in the world. It's recognized throughout cultures, nations, and religions. This is the very place where, centuries later, Solomon would build the First Temple. And Abraham's faith was tested beyond reason in that very place."

"And did Abraham obey?"

"Yes. As a matter of fact, he did." Dr. Abrams slips his glasses back on, running his fingers behind his ear. "Abraham and Isaac made the journey. Isaac carried the wood for the offering. As they climbed the mountain, Isaac asked his father, 'Where is the lamb for the burnt offering?' Abraham replied, 'God Himself will provide the lamb.' *(Genesis 22:7-8)*"

"And did God provide, Dr. Abrams?"

"He certainly did. At the very moment Abraham raised his knife, the Lord called out, 'Do not lay a hand on the boy.' Abraham looked up and saw a ram caught in a thicket. *(Genesis 22:12-13)* The Lord provided, just as Abraham had trusted he would."

Shield hesitates, nodding and scanning the jury. "Dr. Abrams, from your decades of research, does this story hold any significance beyond religious belief?"

"Absolutely. Without question," Dr. Abrams shakes his head, taking a slow sip of water before continuing. "Abraham's story is not just a religious story; it's historical fact. The archaeological record aligns flawlessly with the biblical account. The existence of the Temple Mount, the ancient customs of sacrifice, and the written history of Abraham's descendants all confirm this. Faith and history perfectly align." Dr. Abrams interlocks his fingers back and forth, symbolizing a meshing or cohesion of the account.

"And, Dr. Abrams, what does this story ultimately teach us about Trust?"

"It teaches us that Trust isn't about having all the answers. It's about stepping forward anyway. Abraham Trusted when he couldn't see. He walked forward when the path wasn't clear, when all he could see was desert and emptiness ahead. And in the end? His Trust was not misplaced."

Shield nods, thanking the witness. "No further questions, Your Honor."

Shield moves to the defense table, his shoes echoing with each step. He holds up a photograph of an ancient, weathered stone. "Your Honor, the defense moves to admit *Exhibit 2: The Foundation Stone* into evidence.

61

Christians, Jews, and even Muslims believe this to be the very stone where Abraham was prepared to sacrifice Isaac. It is located on the Temple Mount in Jerusalem, a site revered by billions across the world."

"And what's the significance of this stone?" The judge leans forward, hands interlocked as he taps his index fingers together.

"This stone isn't just a relic. It's a witness. Measuring 13 feet in diameter and carved from the very bedrock of the Temple Mount, this stone has stood for millennia. It ties the story of Abraham to real-world geography and archaeology. This stone serves as evidence that these events are not fairytales or myth but recorded history."

The prosecutor almost knocks his chair over while jumping from his seat. It bounces into the wood separating the gallery and the legal teams. "Objection! Your Honor, the significance of this stone is speculative at best. It's impossible to definitively prove this is the same stone from Abraham's time."

The judge breathes heavily like he's about to blow out his birthday candles. But this is no birthday celebration. He purses his lips together, one side curling higher. "I'll allow the exhibit, but the jury is instructed to weigh its significance carefully."

Shield takes the photo and takes it for a stroll in front of the jury, taking a brief pause in front of each of them. "This stone's existence underscores the enduring legacy of Trust, even if we cannot definitively prove it's the exact site. This act of Trust remains foundational across countless generations, cultures, faiths, and history itself."

Reed springs from his chair, quickly buttons his jacket, and stalks to the witness stand. His prey stares right back at him.

"Dr. Abrams, let's talk about this little Trust exercise, shall we? Just so the jury understands, how many years passed between the time God promised Abraham a son and the time Isaac was actually born?"

"Twenty-five years," Dr. Abrams lays open his hand towards Reed like he's handing him a gift.

"Twenty . . . five . . . *years*," Reed lets out a low whistle, shaking his head. The whistle jumps around the courtroom, penetrating every person's ear space. "That's longer than most marriages last. Imagine someone promises your heart's desire and then is silent for two and a half decades. Is that what you call Trust?"

"Yes. Because God's track record is perfect." Dr. Abrams's eyebrows raise slightly as he tilts his head to the right. "Just because there was a delay in man's eyes doesn't mean the promise was broken. God didn't say you will have a son in one year, two years, or even five years . . . did he? This twenty-five-year delay means the timing had to be right."

"Thank you, Dr. Abrams, but I'll be the one asking the questions." Reed's nostrils flare, his eyes narrowing at Dr. Abrams. His front foot is planted with a hand in his pocket as his irritation shows at Dr. Abrams's ignorance of courtroom etiquette. "Now, speaking of timing, when God didn't seem to hold up his end of the deal, Abraham took matters into his own hands, didn't he? God promised Abraham a son through his wife, Sarah. But when things weren't happening fast enough, he decided to speed up the process himself, didn't he?"

"Yes. Abraham took matters into his own hands." Dr. Abrams pulls his brows together. He frowns, letting out a quick breath. "I would call that a moment of weakness, a flicker of doubt. But even then, God's promise did not waver. God still fulfilled that promise on his timing."

"Ah, so Abraham didn't fully trust." Reed flashes a "Gotcha!" grin. "He doubted. He took matters into his own hands. He didn't believe. And we're supposed to see this Abraham as the pinnacle of Trust?"

"Yes, that's right." Dr. Abrams takes off his glasses and wipes the lenses with his denim shirt. He then points them at Reed, taunting him in an up-and-down motion. "Because Trust isn't about never struggling or never doubting. It's about choosing to believe, even when doubt creeps in."

"So let's fast-forward to when Abraham finally gets his miraculous son." Reed shakes his head and throws his hands up mockingly like he's trying to open the sky. "He's waited twenty-five years. And then, what happens? God asks him to sacrifice him. Dr. Abrams . . . how is that Trustworthy?"

Dr. Abrams takes a deep, calming breath. He leans forward in his chair, looking Reed right in the eyes. "It's because Abraham understood something that we too often forget: God's promises never fail. Abraham believed that even if he sacrificed Isaac, God would raise him from the dead to keep his word."

"And conveniently, Isaac was never actually sacrificed, was he?" Reed lets out a sharp breath through his nose, part exhale, part laugh. Shaking his head, a smirk curls at the corner of his mouth. "So, doesn't that make this whole thing pointless, a horribly meaningless exercise?"

"No, not at all." Dr. Abrams leans back, rocking slightly in the chair. "It wasn't meaningless. It was a picture of something far greater. Abraham's test was a foreshadowing, a preview of the day when another father would offer his son. The only difference is that during this time, there would be no ram in the thicket."

A wave of silence washes over the courtroom.

Reed grinds his teeth, clenching his jaw. He pivots, scrambling like an overworked pasta dough.

"Now Dr. Abrams, you're an archaeologist, a historian, a man of facts. Can you prove beyond a shadow of a doubt that this is the exact stone where Abraham nearly sacrificed Isaac?"

"No," Dr. Abrams shrugs, a brief smile escaping.

"So you admit it's just speculation, a religious assumption?"

"What I can prove is that the historical record aligns definitively with the biblical account. The Temple Mount exists. The region of Moriah exists. The Foundation Stone exists. The traditions and customs of sacrifice have been documented across centuries. Just because we don't have a sign that reads 'Abraham was here' doesn't mean it didn't happen."

"So, what? We're just supposed to trust this?" Reed smirks, mockingly shrugging his shoulders and adjusting his tie.

"Absolutely. Because the evidence supports it."

Reed purses his lips together and frowns. "No further questions." Reed hastily walks back to his seat.

Shield rises one final time for the day and rolls his shoulders back. "Ladies and gentlemen, today we started to expose the real villain in this trial. And it isn't Trust. Remember, Trust didn't just break himself. He was broken. If goodness has an architect, doesn't that prove evil has an author? And his greatest trick? It's deception. Convincing you he doesn't even exist and trying to manipulate you into believing that Trust is the real issue.

"The devil doesn't need you to worship him. He just needs you to stop Trusting in God. That's it. His goal is to convince you that God is distant and unreliable and that he doesn't care. And if he can accomplish that by preying on your colored history with Trust, then even better. By breaking Trust, he breaks humanity. He doesn't need to destroy us; he only needs to convince us to stop Trusting, to stop believing."

Shield pauses, before turning toward the evidence table. "Today, we called Dr. Abrams to the stand, a historian and archaeologist who spent his lifetime studying the Middle Eastern world and the life of Abraham. Abraham, a real man who endured years of waiting, testing, and wrestling with doubt. And through every trial, history confirms that Abraham found God to be faithful and Trustworthy.

"We introduced *Exhibit 1: The Bible* as a historical record of Trust misplaced, Trust restored, and a God with a perfect and proven track record. We showed you *Exhibit 2: The Foundation Stone*, a tangible link to Abraham's story, a historical reminder that these are not myths. They are history."

Shield stops, stepping back. "As you weigh today's testimonies and the evidence before you, ask yourself: Is Trust really the problem, or have we been played by the ultimate manipulator? We've been part of a grand illusion. And we bought it, hook, line, and sinker. We've been blinded by misdirection, like we were neutralized by the *Men in Black*. But now, the curtain's been pulled back. The enemy is exposed. No amount of eye bleach can hide the truth. His illusion is shattered. It's time to stop believing his lies, to hold him accountable, and to reclaim the truth he's so desperate to keep buried."

Shield thanks the jury and returns to his seat.

Judge Steele slams the gavel, "Court is adjourned."

As the jury files out, the defense has left them with some serious soul-searching to do, to confront their own doubts and beliefs. An alternate suspect has been offered by the defense, but will it be enough to sway their opinion?

CHAPTER 5

Trust's Firm Foundation

THE COURTHOUSE STEPS, worn smooth by countless feet, represent the frontline of this legal battle. The biting wind whips and the crisp outdoor air does little to reduce the aftershock of the defense's first day. The crowd outside whizzes like a relentless beehive. Journalists fight over top of one another, pushing and pulling for soundbites, their microphones pointed weapons. Somewhere in the distance, a street musician halfheartedly strums a guitar, bobbing his head, swaying back and forth while the drama unfolds around him.

Curtis Reed stands at the base of the steps, rigid and his briefcase clutched tightly at his side. "Shield!" he barks like an out-of-control, relentless chihuahua.

Harvey Shield emerges from the towering courthouse pillars, shoulders back, his hair blowing in the wind, not a care in the world. And Trust trails behind him like a lost puppy. Shield doesn't respond immediately. He takes his sweet time to adjust his jacket and cufflinks in a mocking display, taking an extra second to brush the lint off the front of his gray jacket before meeting Reed's death stare with a sarcastic smile. Shield's amusement only adds fuel to the fire.

"You're a stubborn man, Shield. A deal was on the table, a good one. But now, here you are, dragging this circus along. You can't honestly believe you've done enough to save Trust?"

"I think the word you're looking for is 'determined,'" Shield laughs, amused at Reed's displeasure. "But I'm flattered you think I'm stubborn, Reed. Truly, I am. I know how hard it is for you to give a compliment."

"Save the wordplay for the courtroom," Reed snaps, his face verging on the color of tomato sauce. "You know as well as I do the jury doesn't like loose ends. Trust is a liability, a ticking time bomb. And when it explodes, he's taking you out with him."

Shield quickly moves close to Reed, almost nosing him. "Funny thing, Reed. The jury doesn't like loose ends. Well, they hate being manipulated even more. And they despise liars." Shield says, adjusting his tie. "Let's just say they're starting to see right through your little act."

"You're digging your own grave, Shield. This is a losing hand."

Shield slowly reaches into his jacket pocket, pulls out a folded note, and presses it into Reed's hand.

"For your eyes only," Shield winks, just slowly enough to invoke a reaction.

Reed opens the note, his fingers clutching the edges. Two words are scribbled on the page: "*Good luck. ;-)*" Reed's face turns different shades of red. He's like an overfilled ballon about to explode. "You'll regret this!"

"Maybe." Shield smiles, mockingly bowing in his direction. "But then again, maybe not. Guess we'll find out soon enough, won't we?"

Shield does an about-face and walks away, Trust racing quickly behind him. Reed squints at them, crumpling the note into a tiny ball of rage as he watches them disappear.

The courtroom is a gladiator's arena of intense debate. Accusations from the prosecution linger in the jurors' minds. Doubt whispers in their ears, feeding on their uncertainty. Trust sits at the defense table. His eyelids are bright red; his eye bags are puffy, swollen. He clenches his jaw, pursing his lips together. He has ink stains on his white shirt. His suit seems to be hanging loosely from his fame, like this trial is now some new weight-loss fad. Facing multiple charges, including possibly being the world's worst investment, will do that to a person. His shoulders sag as he recalls the accusations that have been hurled at him. A risk not worth taking. A gamble no sane person should make. Reckless, unreliable, dangerous even. And now, the most important question demands our attention.

Can anyone, even God, be Trusted?

Everyone in the gallery leans in, holding their breaths. Like the slightest exhale would be a rude interruption to the dramatics. Harvey Shield rises and buttons his jacket. Yesterday had been a day of revelations. The defense began dismantling the prosecution's argument, proving that Trust was not the problem, but rather, where we place our Trust was.

Today, the defense promises to go further, to dig deeper: to prove Trust can be restored and to reveal a completely trustworthy ally.

Shield smooths the front of his jacket and strolls toward the jury. The sounds of his polished shoes reverberate off the four walls of the courtroom.

"Ladies and gentlemen of the jury, we've reached a pivotal moment. The prosecution spent days hurling accusations at the wall, hoping something will stick. They portrayed Trust as a fraud, an accomplice, and a perpetrator of heartbreak and betrayal. But today, we shift the narrative. Today, we address the heart of this trial. The prosecution wants to convince you that Trust is irreparable, that Trust is the source of all our problems, and because of that, that not even God himself cannot be Trusted.

"Today, we will show you that Trust is not the perpetrator, it is the victim. It has been manipulated, abused, and discarded by those who use it for their own selfish gain. Trust is not guilty of fraud or breach of contract. It is an innocent bystander, framed by the very people who failed to uphold the promises they made."

Shield turns, motioning toward Trust. His hand sweeps to reveal the defendant anew. "Look at Trust. What you see is not a criminal but a cornerstone. Trust sits here, not because of his criminal actions but because of injustice. Trust has no agenda, no schemes. He has no dog in this fight. He does not act. Others act upon him. And yet, time and time again, humanity drags Trust into the courtroom of its failures, accusing Trust of crimes it is incapable of committing. The real criminals are those who misuse Trust, those who would twist Trust's nature for their own gain and then discard him when he no longer serves their purpose."

The jury intently focuses on Trust. Their narrowing eyes scan him up and down, inspecting him like he's in the TSA check-in line. He slowly shifts his weight left and right in his seat. His crisp fade is no longer crispy. It's grown out and matches the length of his messy hair on top that's running every which way. He carries the weight of every broken promise and shattered dream on his shoulders. His hands remain folded on the table as he stares back at the jurors. He's here and doesn't plan on going anywhere. This is the fight of his life, and he will endure until the bitter end.

"Yesterday, we showed evidence and presented testimony that Trust, when placed in God, is unshakable and transformative. Today, we take it a step further. We will provide evidence of a God who can be Trusted. We'll show that his attributes, his faithfulness, his unchanging nature make him the ultimate foundation for Trust. While the true criminal is the devil in this trial, we will also definitively prove that when people place their Trust in God, he directs their paths. *Proverbs 3:5–6 tells us, 'Trust in the Lord with all your heart, and lean not on your own understanding; in all your ways acknowledge him, and he shall direct your paths.'*

"Today, we hear from witnesses who experienced God's guidance and faithfulness. We will introduce artifacts into evidence that corroborate the historical accuracy of these events. And we will continue to expose the lies of the enemy who seeks to sow doubt and mistrust in our hearts. Ladies and gentlemen, let's proceed."

Shield walks to the evidence table and lifts a board covered in Scripture. "Your Honor, the defense moves to admit *Exhibit 3: God's Attributes.* This evidence outlines the characteristics of God that prove his trustworthiness. It is not just theology. It is evidence of a God whose promises are reliable, whose character is unchanging, and whose sovereignty governs all things."

The prosecution kicks his seat out and makes his water glass wobble. "Objection, Your Honor. The defense is attempting to turn this courtroom into a church service. Attributes of God? This is opinion, not evidence."

Judge Steele raises his eyebrow. "Response, Counselor?"

"Your Honor, the prosecution did not object when they entered philosophical arguments and emotional testimonies against Trust. They referenced Genesis and several theological principles to make their case. If their arguments are valid, then so are ours. Further, Your Honor, this exhibit is not speculative. It is historical fact, supported by historical records dating back over two thousand years. History attests to this.

"God's attributes recorded in the Bible, in the Dead Sea scrolls themselves are critical to understanding why Trust placed in God is never misplaced."

The judge nods. "Objection overruled. Exhibit 3 is admitted."

Shield turns and walks the board in front of the jury.

"Ladies and gentlemen, let's consider what we know about God's character:

- *He is unchanging*: 'For I am the Lord, I do not change.' (Malachi 3:6)

- He is faithful: 'Your faithfulness endures to all generations.' (Psalm 119:90)

- He is truthful: 'God is not a man, that he should lie.' (Numbers 23:19)

- He is loving: 'The steadfast love of the Lord never ceases; his mercies never come to an end.' (Lamentations 3:22-23)

- He is sovereign: 'The Most High rules in the kingdom of men.' (Daniel 4:17)

"These are not abstract ideas. They are truths experienced by those who place their Trust in him. This is the essence of who God is. And through them, we see that Trust placed in God is not a gamble. It is a guarantee."

Harvey Shield, charged with excitement, places the board on an easel in front of the jury and moves to the center of the room. "Ladies and gentlemen, today we introduce someone who stood against impossible odds. A man who faced a giant. A man who looked fear, doubt, and overwhelming circumstances in the eyes. A soldier. A warrior. A survivor."

Shield gestures toward the courtroom doors. "The defense calls Staff Sergeant Daniel Mercer."

A uniformed man in his mid-thirties sporting a high and tight ducks under the double doors and marches in. He holds his camouflage cap, tucking it into the crease of his arm like he's holding a football. He has a large scar tracing down the right side of his face, hugging close to his sideburns. His gait is confident, deliberate.

The gallery leans in.

Mercer takes the stand and raises his right hand.

"Do you swear to tell the truth, the whole truth, and nothing but the truth?" the bailiff asks.

"I do," Mercer's voice booms through the courtroom, rattling the eardrums of the jury.

Shield steps closer. "Sergeant Mercer, can you tell the court what happened the day of October 12, 2005?"

"We were ten klicks east of Baghdad. My unit was conducting a recon mission in hostile territory." Mercer tightens his jaw, his brows tightly pinched together. "Things went south. Real fast. The enemy ambushed us. A suicide bomber ran out in front of our unit and the explosion closed us in. The shrapnel from the explosion gave me this souvenir." He waves his two fingers up and down the side of his face where his scar is prominently displayed. "During the chaos, I got separated and my radio was destroyed. Blood was dripping down my face. I could barely see out of my right eye. In that moment, I thought I was half blind. I wiped my face with the sleeve of my cammis and once the blur subsided, I looked around and I was all alone. All I had was my sidearm, a combat knife, and a canteen for water."

The jury sits motionless, eyes locked on Sergeant Mercer, barely blinking. A hushed stillness clings to the room, the kind that makes you choke on the air. A few lean forward, elbows resting on their knees, hands clasped like a lifeline. No one fidgets, no one checks the clock, and everyone leans in, entranced by the moment.

"So, let me make sure I understand. You were separated from your unit. You were bleeding. Blinded. Outnumbered. Outgunned. No hope of survival. What did you do?"

"I remembered my training, my faith," Mercer shakes his head staring right at the jurors. "The stories my grandfather used to tell me raced through my mind, playing on a loop. One in particular, David and Goliath, played over and over again."

Shield leans in. "David and Goliath? What do you mean?"

"So, there's this story of a kid with a slingshot fighting a massive giant with a sword. When you're little, those stories charge your batteries. You dress up, you make figures, you reenact the scene as best you can. I used to go outside with my Swiss army knife and shave some sticks down and wrap nylon around them to make a slingshot. Then I would shoot at random trees, envisioning them toppling over just like the giant. You see, in the story of David and Goliath, he trusted something bigger than himself. He did something that seemed foreign to a lot of us. He believed and trusted that he was equipped with everything he needed. The obstacle in front of him was impossible; it was in the way. So, I did the same thing. I stopped thinking about the negatives. I didn't throw a pity party. I didn't panic. I searched for places to hide and rummaged through bins to conceal my identity. I focused on my training and trusted I would find a way out.

"Survival is next to impossible." Mercer looks over at the jury. "Anytime a soldier is trapped behind enemy lines, the chances of survival are grim. Slim to none. It's less than ideal."

"Let's talk about what happened next."

"I found a spot underneath some rubble and carefully arranged my body to remain hidden. I grabbed handfuls of dirt, rocks, anything I could find to better conceal my location. And I waited. Nightfall was my friend, and I hid there for what seemed like ages. The minutes stretched on as I bided my time. Once it was pitch black outside and I could hear the faint sound of music and saw the dancing of flames in the distant windows, I knew that was my opportunity. I inched out of my hiding spot, crawling on my hands and knees, careful not to make a sound. Once I got around the other side of the rubble, crouching close to the ground, my knees almost dragging on the dust, I saw them. There were five hostiles grouped together."

Mercer takes a deep breath, his gaze never leaving the direction of the jury. "There was one surefire way out of that hellhole, and my escape route was blocked. I had one shot, and I had to take it." Mercer reaches down to his right and picks up a metaphorical rock. "I grabbed some pebbles and tossed them in their direction and hid close to the rubble. The hostiles sent one of their peons over, and once he got close enough, I snatched him up by the neck and neutralized him. As I laid him on the ground out of sight, I reached down and grabbed his rifle. I moved behind an abandoned car nearby. Three more approached. I crawled on the ground and posted near the front tire. As soon as they were in sight, I took them out. Blap, blap, blap."

Mercer offsets his hands three inches from each other and shoots the wall as though it were the enemy. "Three shots and they were neutralized. But the last one?" Mercer pauses. "As soon as he heard the gunshots, he ran. I gave away my position and had to move, fast."

"What did you do?"

"I didn't hesitate. I assessed my surroundings and looked for a tactical advantage. As I moved through the town, I peered around corners and vehicles. On my toes as I searched for the remaining hostile, I pivoted around one building and there he was! He was crouched between a wooden post, his weapon drawn in my direction. I barely could see him, but there was a light across the street that lit him up like a painted laser. I doubled back and came around in the opposite direction. I crawled on the ground, picked up some loose gravel, and threw it to my left. He rose up and fired at the air. Once he was exposed, it was game over. I had him."

"Staff Sergeant Mercer, you took out five enemies by yourself as you fought to stay alive. You said you trusted your training. You focused on the moment, the task at hand. Was there anything else that helped you stay alive?"

"I focused on the objective. I thought about the positives. I stopped trying to win on my own. I trusted. I believed. Just like David who stood before a giant with nothing but a slingshot and a handful of stones. And faith. His faith was my faith, and I just kept picturing seeing my family one more time."

Shield pauses, his arms folded at his chest, and taps his right index finger on his chin, letting the testimony simmer. "Your Honor, the defense introduces *Exhibit 4: The Account of David and Goliath.*" Shield gestures toward the screen as an ancient battlefield flashes.

"This is the historical record of another soldier. A young man, like Sergeant Mercer, who stood against impossible odds. A boy who faced an enemy that had crippled armies with fear. And, like Sergeant Mercer, this young man did the unthinkable. Many of you have heard this story before. Sports broadcasters love bringing up David vs. Goliath."

He turns to Mercer. "Sergeant, would you do the honors?"

"'*A champion named Goliath came out from the Philistine camp . . . over nine feet tall. For forty days, he taunted the armies of Israel. No one dared to fight him.*'"

Shield stops Mercer, glancing at the jury. "Sound familiar?"

"'*Then came a shepherd boy named David, with no armor and no sword. Just five stones, a sling, and faith in the God who never fails. While the warriors cowered, David stood tall. "While the army hesitated, David ran toward the battle. And with one stone . . . the giant fell.*' (1 Samuel 17: 23-50)"

Shield steps forward. "And David? He knew what it meant to Trust when everything and everyone said he shouldn't."

The soldier nods, his brows pulling down and together.

Shield faces the jury. "Ladies and gentlemen, David's story is not a fairytale. It's history. It's one of history's greatest battlefields. You heard the testimony of a man who lived it, a soldier stranded behind enemy lines who fought against his own Goliath and survived. And in doing so, we are reminded of a simple truth: Trust isn't about certainty. It's about where you place it."

Shield approaches the evidence table, his leather shoes clacking as he makes his way. He pulls out a series of images and archaeological reports from his briefcase and sets them down on the defense table for display. "Your Honor, the defense introduces *Exhibit 5: Artifacts of Gath and the Philistines.* These artifacts include the excavation findings of the ancient city of Gath, the home of Goliath. These artifacts authenticate the historical account and the accuracy of the Philistine civilization."

The judge nods. "Proceed."

Shield faces the jury, holding up a photograph of a massive stone wall. "Ladies and gentlemen, these are the remnants of the city of Gath. Uncovered by archaeologists in modern-day Tell es-Safi. The dimensions of the city wall are staggering. Some of these stones measure over twelve feet and weigh several tons. This was not just any city; it was a fortress, a stronghold.

"Gath was home to the Philistines, a people infamous in ancient history and frequently mentioned in the Bible. Among its most well-known residents was Goliath, the giant warrior who stood over nine feet tall. Armed with weapons so massive that only a man of great stature could wield them."

Shield points to an enlarged diagram of a Philistine sword excavated near the site. "This artifact, a bronze sword, measures nearly four feet, an indicator of the extraordinary size and strength of its wielder. Artifacts such as this provide context to the biblical account of David and Goliath as a historical event."

The prosecutor stands. "Objection, Your Honor! The defense is attempting to pass off incomplete archaeological findings as definitive proof of their narrative. The existence of a city or a large man doesn't validate every detail of the Bible's account."

Judge raises his hand in the direction of Reed. "Sustained, in part. Counsel, you may continue, but remember that the jury is tasked with interpreting the evidence themselves."

"Ladies and gentlemen, our goal here is not to prove every detail beyond a shadow of a doubt but rather to show the historical and archaeological credibility of the context surrounding David's testimony. No further questions."

Reed wastes little time, speeding to the witness stand while his jacket blows up behind him. He invades Sergeant Mercer's space.

"Sergeant Mercer, thank you for your service. You truly survived the impossible. Trapped behind enemy lines, outnumbered, and hunted. Yet you made it out."

"That's right."

"But what happened after you made it home? Was the hero's welcome all it was cracked up to be?"

"War changes a man," Mercer grits his teeth, his lips curling downward. "It takes time to adjust."

"Adjust. Right. That's an interesting way of saying that everything started to fall apart, isn't it?"

Shield stands, "Objection, Your Honor. Badgering the witness?" His hands raised at his sides.

"Sustained. Counselor, watch it. I will not have you disrespecting a veteran of the Armed Services in my courtroom."

"Apologies, Your Honor. I'll rephrase. Sergeant Mercer, you were unfaithful to your wife, weren't you? Just like David, the man you've been compared to. This David went on to betray one of his own men. David took what wasn't his. And so did you."

Mercer looks down, his hands balled together as he deeply sighs. "Yes," he growls through his teeth.

"Here's the thing about Trust. It's easy to claim it on the battlefield, isn't it? When the bullets are flying, when the mission is clear, when survival is on the line. But when life slows down and the real battles begin, you fell apart."

"I made mistakes."

"Mistakes," Reed mockingly shoots out a short breath from between his lips. "You destroyed your family. The same family you were fighting to get home to. The same people who prayed for your safe return. You weren't Trustworthy at all, were you?"

"I failed. I don't deny that. I'm human. But failure doesn't erase everything that came before it."

"Doesn't it, though? The moment you betrayed your family, Trust was shattered. And once Trust is broken, it can ever really be put back together. Let's fast forward, shall we? You get promoted. You're given command, a second chance. But then—" Reed pauses. "Your unit gets attacked. Soldiers under your command died. Young men who Trusted you to bring them home."

Mercer grimaces, his nose wrinkling hard.

"You Trusted your instincts, didn't you? You thought you were leading them to safety. Instead, you led them straight into a trap, an ambush."

"I Trusted the intel we had," Mercer's nostrils flare.

"But it was wrong, wasn't it? You Trusted something and it failed you. And your men paid the ultimate price. Just like Trust has failed countless others in this very courtroom."

Reed steps closer, lowering his voice. "Tell me, Sergeant. After everything—the war, the betrayal, after the failures, do you still Trust as blindly as you did back then?"

"I do," Mercer meets Reed's gaze head-on. "I Trust because of what I've been through. Not in the same way. Not in myself. Not in flawed intel. But I Trust in something greater than me. I Trusted, and I made it out. When everything else fell apart. When I fell apart. Trust and faith were the only things remaining."

Reed smirks, turning to the jury. "Ladies and gentlemen, do you really want to gamble with Trust? Trust in flawed leaders, in flawed intelligence, in flawed men? Even a war hero who admits he got it wrong. Can the world really afford to keep making the same mistakes? No further questions, Your Honor."

Mr. Shield adjusts his tie and approaches. "Your Honor, the defense calls our next witnesses: three university students who refused to bend the knee when the world demanded their silence."

The gallery stirs with whispers and frantically shaking heads.

From the back of the courtroom, three figures rise and step out into the aisle. Shane leads the pack and is average height and build with a short crewcut, a blue polo shirt, and khakis. Next, Michael walks behind him. His longer blond hair is brushed back and waves at the gallery with each step. He's wearing a teal button-down shirt, untucked and covering the back of denim jeans, as his black Chucks squeak on the flooring. Anchoring these witnesses is Ezra, a little taller than the other two and wearing a red Hawaiian shirt and gray jeans.

Mr. Shield gestures toward the three witnesses as they take their seats at the witness stand. "Ladies and gentlemen, meet Shane, Michael, and Ezra—three students at one of the country's most prestigious universities, three students who were told to stay silent, to fall in line, to ignore what they thought was right or be thrown into the fire."

Shield paces, beginning to wear a hole in the section of flooring in front of the jury with his hands folded behind his back. "Shane, let's start at the beginning. Can you tell us what happened?"

Shane leans forward, rubbing his hand quickly back and forth over his short hair. "There's nothing special about us. We're students just like everyone else. But when the anti-Israel protests erupted across campus, the administration gave us two choices: join or ignore."

Michael, seated beside him, crosses his arms. "We weren't against peaceful protests that are protected by the Constitution. But we were against the lies, the hateful rhetoric that went beyond their so-called activism. It wasn't about dialogue. It was about control. And when we refused to fall in line? That's when things started to get ugly."

Ezra leans back, shaking his head. "They told us our futures were over, that we'd never work in our fields, that we'd be blacklisted in our careers.

Professors who encouraged free thought now warned us '*You don't want to be on the wrong side of this.*'"

Shield nods. "And what did you do?"

"We held the line. We stood firm. We didn't bow. When the next protest happened, we stood in unity, in opposition. We stood across from them in the field, holding our Bibles in one arm and locking arms with the other," Shane responds.

"And what happened next?"

"They started pushing us. Spitting on us. Bumping up close to us, in our faces. Lunging forward and cussing at us. They couldn't believe we were standing with them, supporting their position. But we didn't budge. We held the line. Even though they were trying to instigate a situation, we steadied ourselves. The louder they shouted in our faces, the more we dug our heels in on that grassy hill. And the backlash was intense, immediate. People in the crown recorded the event, mostly focusing on us standing in the way of their protest. And then it made its way into the hands of the administration. And they dragged us through the mud. They branded us as extremists, racists, traitors. Some of our classmates refused to speak to us. No one talked to us, sat with us at lunch. People would purposefully shoulder us in the hallways. I know I dropped a book or two during those encounters. And when that wasn't enough, they really turned up the heat."

Ezra leans in. "They said we were creating a hostile environment. We were called into the Dean's office and given ultimatums. 'Apologize. Abandon your beliefs. Distance yourselves from your stance, or you're finished.' They threatened to suspend us, possibly even expel us."

Shield steps closer. "And yet, here you are."

"We were thrown into the fire," Shane smiles. "The administration wanted to make an example out of us. We were ridiculed, targeted, put through hearings. But we didn't stand alone."

Michael's eyes flicker at his friends before focusing on the jury. "No. Just like in the furnace long ago, there was another with us."

Ezra's voice rises with conviction. "While we were going through this, it reminded us of Shadrach, Meshach, and Abed-Nego. These men opposed the leader of their day and refused to budge from their beliefs. And when they faced certain death, they stood strong. And God didn't just bring them through it. He stood with them in the flames. And that's exactly what happened with us. We prayed, we sought the Lord, and the more we were pressured, the more we stood our ground. We felt God was right there with us, encouraging us, leading us through the fire."

Shield approaches the jury. "These three students refused to bow. They refused to abandon their beliefs. Just like Shadrach, Meshach, and Abed-Nego before them, they risked their standing in the school, their very futures. They risked everything. They Trusted in something greater. They Trusted in God. And he showed up in a powerful way."

Shield takes a momentary pause. He walks to the evidence table and holds up a series of photographs and documents. "Your Honor, the defense introduces *Exhibit 6: Babylonian Artifacts* into evidence. These Babylonian artifacts include kiln-fired bricks inscribed with King Nebuchadnezzar's name and records of Babylonian furnace construction, which corroborate the historical accuracy and cultural setting described in Daniel's account."

"Proceed, Counselor," Judge Steele swipes to the left.

"These artifacts were found across archaeological sites in Babylon, modern-day Iraq. The evidence shows massive kiln structures used for brick-making under Nebuchadnezzar's reign. These align with the biblical narrative of the fiery furnace described in Daniel 3, where Hananiah, Mishael, and Azariah faced execution for refusing to bow to the king's golden image."

Shield holds up a high-resolution image of a kiln-fired brick, featuring an inscription that reads, "*Nebuchadnezzar, King of Babylon*," and walks it in front of the jury. Their eyes don't falter from the photograph as Shield takes the time to give each one a moment to inspect.

"Your Honor, this inscription authenticates Nebuchadnezzar's existence and links him to the industrial-scale kilns described in Scripture. These furnaces that reached temperatures capable of producing bricks for the Babylonian empire were no mere embellishment. Their existence is verifiable; they were lethal and pivotal in maintaining Babylonian authority."

Reed stands. "Objection, Your Honor. The defense is attempting to blur the line between historical artifacts and divine intervention. A brick with Nebuchadnezzar's name proves nothing about the supernatural events described in Daniel."

"Sustained. Counsel, please stick to the facts when presenting historical context unless you can directly tie this exhibit to the claims of your witnesses."

Shield nods. "Understood, Your Honor."

Turning back to the jury, Shield continues, "Ladies and gentlemen, the purpose of this exhibit is not to prove the miraculous, only to establish the historical credibility of the events. These kilns were real. The execution method they facilitated was terrifyingly effective, and Nebuchadnezzar's authority over such acts is indisputable fact."

Reed pushes back his chair and stalks toward the three students.

"Shane, Michael, Ezra, you claim that you stood against overwhelming pressure, risking your academic and professional futures for the sake of your beliefs. That's a very compelling story. But let me ask you this: was it truly faith that carried you through, or was it just reckless youth?"

"We didn't stand our ground to prove a point," Shane says, sitting up straight and slamming his fist on his leg. "We stood because compromising meant denying what we knew to be true."

Reed nods. "Right, right. That's noble of you. But let's talk consequences. You say you were 'thrown into the fire.' That you were ostracized, blacklisted, threatened with expulsion. But did any of that actually happen? Or were these just scare tactics, designed to make you uncomfortable? Because last I checked, no one's throwing students into furnaces these days."

Michael leans forward. "We were called into disciplinary hearings. Professors told us we'd ruined our careers before they even began. Classmates who used to call us friends shunned us. People smeared our names online. The comments on the videos they recorded were horrific. If you think that's just 'uncomfortable,' you've never had the world turn against you overnight."

"So you were criticized, canceled," Reed smirks. "Welcome to the internet. It happens every day. But let's be honest, was this really about faith? Or was it about pride? The refusal to admit that maybe you picked the wrong hill to die on?"

Ezra stares at Reed, clenching his jaw and grinding his teeth. "We weren't looking for a hill to die on. We weren't looking to go viral or make some kind of name for ourselves. But when the world told us to bow, we knew there was only one answer."

"All right, let's talk about this so-called 'fourth figure in the fire.' You claim God stood with you in your trial. But let's be real: was it God . . . or just good timing? You didn't see God, did you? He didn't speak to you, did He?"

Shane raises an eyebrow. "You think walking through the worst moments of your life and coming out stronger is coincidence? No, we didn't see him. No, we didn't hear him. But that doesn't mean we didn't see his fingerprints on the situation. It doesn't mean we didn't feel a strong pull toward certain decisions."

Reed shrugs. "Hey, people face hardship all the time and make it through. That doesn't mean they had backup. Maybe you just had supporters. Maybe some sympathetic faculty members fought for you behind the scenes. Maybe public pressure kept the administration from pulling the trigger. Did you ever consider that?"

"No one fought for us. No one backed us up." Michael folds his arm, shaking his head. "If anything, we were pushed harder. But we weren't alone. Not even for a second."

"Oh, isn't that convenient? An invisible protector," Reed grins. "You say God was there, but where's the proof?"

Ezra tilts his head down and glares at Reed. "The fact that we're here, that we walked through the fire and didn't fold is proof enough."

"Or maybe it's just a story. A useful tale, wrapped up in a neat package to justify your actions." He turns sharply. "No further questions, Your Honor."

Shield stands once more and approaches the jury. "Ladies and gentlemen, these witnesses show us what it means to trust in God. During intense and life-threatening situations, they put their Trust in the Most High instead of human strength.

"Psalms 115:11 tells us, 'You who fear the Lord, Trust in the Lord; he is their help and their shield.' Each of these witnesses testified how God helped them, shielded them, turning impossible circumstances into moments of triumph. These witnesses teach us something the prosecution doesn't want you to see: that Trust in God doesn't guarantee an easy path. It doesn't mean you'll avoid giants or flames. But it does mean that God will stand with you, guiding your steps, proving his faithfulness over and over again. Their Trust became a lifeline, something stronger than fear and uncertainty."

"Before we adjourn, I leave you with this: If a soldier trapped behind enemy lines could Trust God against his Goliath and three young college students could Trust him in the flames, what's holding you back from Trusting?

Judge Steele's gavel falls, ending today's proceedings. "Court is adjourned."

CHAPTER 6

Trust's Final Stand

WE'VE OFFICIALLY HIT ROUND TWELVE of this heavyweight fight. The prosecution, the defense, the jury, and even the stenographer who stopped pretending to care somewhere around lunchtime on Day Three are feeling the effects. Even Judge Steele looks a little worse for wear. He's probably wondering who he upset to get saddled with this. But today, the air feels denser, suffocating even. Every creak of the wooden benches, every shuffle of papers seems to amplify the stress.

This is it. The defense's final day to make their case. No warm-ups. No takebacksies. No do-overs. How will it all end?

Trust sits at the center of it all. His face looks like it was stung by a bee. His eyes are barely open, his eyelids puffy. His face looks like a sponge, retaining all the water. His shirt collar has gray staining around the rim like it hasn't been washed in a dog's age. His tie loosely hangs, his unbuttoned top shirt button showing through. Trust sits accused of everything but insider trading. (Although Reed might amend that to the charges during his closing argument.) Yet somehow, he's still here, still hanging on. Trust looks over at the jury, searching for some form of understanding, maybe even hope. And today, the defense has one last chance to prove that Trust is worth saving. No pressure, Shield.

Curtis Reed lounges against the table. His black pinstripe suit absorbs the light. Reed's constant need for approval and attention makes him the ultimate one-upper.

Harvey Shield stands opposite of Reed. His navy blue suit is slightly wrinkled from the long drive to the courthouse. Shield locks eyes with Reed, offering a subtle head nod, acknowledging the fight they've been through.

Reed, of course, doesn't return it. That's not in his nature. He smooths his tie and runs a hand through his hair, making sure it is still neat. A silent battle of ego, willpower, and stubbornness rages on. No words are spoken, but the message is clear: *Reed's posture screams certainty. Shields whispers, "Try me."*

The entire courtroom holds their breath like they're lying on the bottom of a pool, every eye locked on Shield as he rises. He does his usual song and dance, adjusting his tie, buttoning his jacket. His gaze sweeps over the jury, lingering on each juror.

"Ladies and gentlemen of the jury, today we conclude our defense of Trust. We will continue to prove that the true criminal in this trial is not Trust. There is a cunning enemy scheming to shift the blame. There is humanity's misuse and haphazard abuse of Trust. They don't deal with him delicately but with reckless abandon.

"To illustrate this, we will call two witnesses today: one who endured unimaginable suffering and never wavered in his Trust, and another who offers a resounding criticism of humanity's tendency to place God on trial rather than confront our own guilt. We will also introduce additional evidence that highlights the redemptive power of placing Trust in the right hands. And finally, we will prove the undeniable historical fact of the Cross."

Shield faces the judge. "Your Honor, the defense calls its next witness, James Harrison."

The gallery turns in unison, anticipating the next witness to pass through these double doors. Only the sound of the humming lights and shifting butts in seats interrupts the still silence. James Harrison, a man in his fifties with black hair and a scraggly black and gray beard, walks in. He's wearing a black tee shirt tucked into his gray camouflage pants. His black leather boots echo as he charts his path to the witness stand. He looks straight ahead, his eyes razor sharp and unblinking, locked onto the witness stand.

Shield approaches. "Mr. Harrison, thank you for being here today. Can you please tell the court what happened to you?"

"It started with the storm," James clears his throat, a loud gulp echoing into the microphone. "It was a category five. We barely had any warning. There was no mercy. The storm turned on a dime and headed right for us. We didn't have time to evacuate. One minute, I had a home, a business, a family under one roof. The next, I was standing in knee-deep water, watching my entire life washed away by the water. The sandbags were like putting a Band-Aid on a shotgun blast. Nothing could've stopped the water from coming in. And the water kept coming, rushing over the sandbags and into the house. We had to retreat upstairs until it passed. There was so much water, so much devastation. The amount of water that dumped in our area created mudslides that obliterated everything in its path."

"And what happened next?"

"Everything was gone. My house? Unlivable, inhumane. My truck? Completely encased in a casket of mud." James breathes heavily through his nostrils, shaking his head back and forth. "There was literally nothing we could do."

The jurors are dialed in, absorbing the devastation and hopelessness of the testimony.

"And then came the aftermath," James continues. "No power. No water. No help in sight. We were displaced, forgotten."

"Mr. Harrison, that kind of loss must have tested your faith."

"I was broken, devastated even. I didn't just question God. I demanded answers. 'Why me? Why my family? What did I do to deserve this?' And all I got was silence."

"And yet, you still held on?"

"Held on?" James nods, clutching his hands behind his head. "Barely. I wrestled with God. I screamed at Him. In my anger and questioning, I remembered Job and his words from the Bible. 'Though he slay me, yet will I trust him' (Job 13:15). 'I know that you can do all things, and that no purpose of yours can be thwarted' (Job 42:2). And I thought, 'If Job could Trust even in the midst of so much suffering, then so can I.'"

"You said you received no answers at first." Shield clasps his hands together. "But then?"

"Then," James chuckles, shaking his head, "Then came the rebuilding. I lost everything and somehow, I gained more. My community? They showed up. People I didn't even know helped clear the debris, donated food, and gave their own money to help us rebuild. Strangers felt like family. And my business? Somehow, we reopened bigger, better. I got back everything I lost—twice as much. I don't even know how that's possible."

"James, what would you say to those who claim that your survival, your restoration, was just dumb luck? That there was no divine intervention?"

"I'd say they don't know what they're talking about," James grins. "They don't understand the odds we were up against. You don't 'luck' your way out of it. No, sir. That was God. He didn't stop the storm, but he stood with me through it. And when it was over? He restored what was lost, and then some."

Shield turns to the jury. "Ladies and gentlemen, James Harrison's story isn't one of blind faith. It's one of tested Trust. He didn't ignore his pain. He didn't deny his doubt. He was angry with God. He questioned, he even screamed at him. But through it all, he never let go. He believed that God had a bigger plan, a purpose even in the midst of his suffering. And in the end?" He gestures to James. "God didn't just bring him through it. He blessed him twice over."

Shield steps back, letting the testimony sink in. "No further questions, Your Honor."

Curtis Reed rises, straightens his suit, smooths his tie, and strides toward James Harrison like a shark circling his prey.

"Mr. Harrison, I remember seeing the carnage on the news. Just devastating," Reed shakes his head, oozing compassion for the witness. "Now you claim that God restored you. That after losing everything, you were, what? Made whole? Given some divine 'second chance'?" He chuckles. "Tell me, does restoration erase the scars? Does it bring back the home you lost? The friends who didn't make it? The sleepless nights spent wondering if you'd ever make it through?"

"No, of course not. It doesn't erase the scars." James rubs his hand up and down across his forearm. "But scars tell a story. And these scars speak of survival, of provision, and of a God who never left, even when the storm took everything else."

"Meaning—that's the magic word, right? Meaning—a way to justify the suffering, to disguise it as something else other than chaos. Tell me, Mr. Harrison, what about the people who didn't make it? Your neighbors, your friends, where was God's sovereignty when they drowned? When they were buried under the wreckage? Did they not Trust him enough? Or were they just . . . unlucky?"

A quiet commotion ripples through the courtroom.

"The Lord gives, and the Lord takes away," James sighs, looking down. "No one is promised tomorrow. But that doesn't mean God isn't in control. My friends' lives were his before they were ours, and he called them home. I mourn them. I miss them. But their loss doesn't make God untrustworthy."

"A God that allows his faithful servant to lose everything. Is that really a God worth Trusting? Doesn't your story actually prove that Trusting God is a gamble at best and a betrayal at worst?"

"If Trusting God is a gamble, then it's the only one worth taking. Because here's what you don't understand. My trust wasn't in my house, my possessions, or my own strength. My Trust was in him. When everything else failed, he didn't."

"You say your suffering brought you closer to God. But couldn't it just as easily have driven you away? Wouldn't it have been more reasonable to curse him and move on?"

"Reasonable by whose standards?" James lets out a half-sigh, half-laugh from his upturned lips. "Yours? The world's? I had my questions. I had my doubts. I brought my pain before him. You want to talk about reasonable? The most unreasonable thing I could have done was walk away from the only one who could carry me through it."

Reed clears his throat. "No further questions."

Shield steps forward and addresses the court. "Your Honor, the defense calls its final witness, Dr. Malcolm Lionheart."

Side whispers and aggressive heads are thrown all throughout the courtroom. Commotion interrupts the proceedings as the renowned Christian philosopher and former atheist steps through one of the doors. Dr. Lionheart, a man in his sixties sporting a tweed jacket and silver-rimmed glasses, strolls in. His hair is combed back and it's been retreating toward the back of his skull for some time now. Dr. Lionheart enters the witness stand and swears the oath before taking his seat in the witness stand.

"Dr. Lionheart, thank you for taking time out of your schedule to be here today. Can you please tell the court your occupation?

"Certainly. I am an author and a philosopher of theology."

"Thank you. Now, Dr. Lionheart, you used to be an atheist, is that correct? Can you please tell the court about those beliefs?"

"I was, at this time, living like so many atheists or antitheists, in a whirl of contradictions. I maintained that God did not exist." Dr. Lionheart adjusts his glasses. "I was also very angry with God for not existing. I was equally angry with him for creating a world."[1]

"Why were you angry with God if you didn't believe in the existence of God?"

"Atheists express their rage against God, although in their view, he does not exist.[2] My argument against God was that the universe seemed so cruel and unjust. But how had I got this idea of just and unjust? A man does

1. (Lewis, A Mind Awake: An Anthology of C. S. Lewis, 61)
2. (Lewis, The Problem of Pain 1940)

not call a line crooked unless he has some idea of a straight line. What was I comparing this universe with when I called it unjust?"[3]

"Dr. Lionheart, what happened? What was the turning point? Was there something specific that led to your change of heart?"

"Atheism turned out to be too simple. If the whole universe has no meaning, we should never have found out that it has no meaning. Through my years of searching and studying, there is no philosophical theory I have yet come across that is a radical improvement on the words of Genesis, 'In the beginning, God made heaven and earth.'"[4]

"Dr. Lionheart, these discoveries impacted your views on faith. In fact, you have written extensively on the human condition and man's relationship with God. Can you share your thoughts on how humanity approaches the idea of Trust and sin?"

"The greatest barrier I have met is the almost total absence of any sense of sin. In ancient times, people approached God as the accused approached a judge. But in modern times, the roles have reversed. Man has placed himself on the bench and put God in the dock. Modern man is quite a kindly judge, ready to acquit God if he provides a reasonable defense for war, poverty, and disease. But the real issue is not God's goodness, it is man's refusal to confront his own guilt. Until we acknowledge the unwelcome diagnosis, we cannot accept the remedy."[5]

Shield turns to the jury. "Ladies and gentlemen, do you hear what Dr. Lionheart is saying? The prosecution wants you to blame Trust and even God for the pain and suffering in the world. But the real issue is neither Trust nor God. It is humanity's refusal to acknowledge our own role in breaking Trust and introducing sin. We are the ones who have misused Trust. And we have the audacity to put Trust and even God on trial. No further questions."

Mr. Reed stands with his usual aura of smugness. He adjusts his suit and tie and approaches the stand. Trust leans forward, refusing to blink, focused on the final line of questioning.

"Dr. Lionheart, you've offered some thought-provoking observations about humanity and trust. You've claimed that modern man has placed God 'in the dock,' as you so eloquently put it. But let's address the core of

3. (Lewis, The Joyful Christian, 7)
4. (Lewis, A Mind Awake: An Anthology of C. S. Lewis, 80)
5. (Lewis, God in the Dock: Essays on Theology and Ethics, 123 - 124)

your argument. Are you saying that the prosecution, and by extension, the jury has no right to question God's trustworthiness?"

"Not at all, sir. Questioning is natural, even necessary." A creeping smile begins to slowly form across Dr. Lionheart's lips. "But the problem arises when questioning becomes presumption. When humanity assumes the role of judge over God, it blinds itself to the deeper truths of its own condition."

"Deeper truths? Let's explore that. If God is so trustworthy, why is the world he created engrossed in suffering? Why do wars rage? Why do children starve? Why do diseases devastate? Isn't it reasonable to hold God accountable?"

"Reasonable, perhaps, but ultimately misguided. The presence of suffering is not a testament to God's untrustworthiness. It is a direct reflection of humanity's rebellion. God, in His infinite wisdom, gave us free will. And with that freedom, we introduced sin into his perfect creation. The real question, then, is not why suffering exists. It's why a holy and just God would continue to extend grace to creatures so hell-bent on their own destruction."

"And yet, Mr. Lionheart, you suggest that humanity is the one on trial, not God." Reed starts wearing a hole in the floor like he's doing the chicken strut while pursing his lips together. "But isn't it fair to ask, if God truly cared, wouldn't he intervene to prevent such atrocities? Wouldn't a Trustworthy God do everything in his power to protect his creation?"

"Let me answer your question with another. What kind of world would you have God create? One without suffering? Without free will? Without consequence? A world where humanity cannot make choices, even terrible ones, would not be a world of Trust or love. It would be a world of robots and puppets enslaved to a divine puppeteer. Trust, real Trust, cannot exist without freedom. And freedom inevitably carries risk."

"Risk, you say." Reed rolls his eyes like a teenager. "But isn't it God's responsibility to mitigate that risk? Shouldn't he, if he truly cared, protect humanity from its own failures?"

A slight pause. Every eye focuses on the exchange.

"You misunderstand the nature of Trust and the nature of God, Counselor. Trust is not about eliminating risk. It is about choosing to believe, despite it. And God has not left us to flounder in our failures. He entered into our suffering. He took on flesh and bore the weight of humanity's sin at the Cross. You ask why God doesn't intervene. I would argue, he already has—in the most profound and sacrificial way possible."

"The Cross is your argument? And yet, here we are, thousands of years later, still plagued by the same suffering and evil. How can you argue it was enough?"

"The Cross was not about eliminating temporal suffering. It was about addressing the eternal condition of the soul. It was God's ultimate act of trustworthiness, offering redemption to a world that had rejected him. And this brings us to a central truth: Jesus Christ. For if he is who he claimed to be, then all your arguments against God's trustworthiness fall apart."

"And what exactly are you claiming, Dr. Lionheart? That Jesus is beyond reproach?" Reed crosses his arms. "That we should simply accept Hhm as trustworthy without question?"

"I am claiming that Jesus left us with only three options. He is either a lunatic, on the level of a man who claims to be a poached egg; a liar, deliberately deceiving billions; or he is exactly who he claimed to be, Lord. There is no middle ground. No reasonable person can dismiss him as merely a great moral teacher. He did not leave us that option."[6]

The courtroom sits in stunned silence. Even Reed seems at a loss for words.

Trust mouths the word, "Boom!" from his seat, understanding the epic mic drop of this moment.

Shield rises and addresses Judge Steele. "Redirect, Your Honor."

Judge Steele motions with two fingers, "Proceed, Counselor."

"Dr. Lionheart, let's return to the question posed by the prosecution: why doesn't God intervene in every instance of suffering? Can you provide an analogy to help the jury better understand this?"

"Imagine, if you will, a parent raising a child. A loving parent does not shield their child from every scrape, every failure, every heartbreak. Why? Because the child would never grow. Suffering, as much as we abhor it, shapes us. It teaches us, refines us, and often leads us to something greater."

"So, you're suggesting that Trust and suffering are connected?"

"Precisely. True Trust is not forged in the absence of adversity but in the midst of it. And God, in his infinite wisdom, uses even our suffering to draw us closer to Him. It is not evidence of his untrustworthiness. It is evidence of his redemptive purpose."

"Thank you, Dr. Lionheart. No further questions."

6. (Lewis, Mere Chritianity, 32)

Throughout the course of Dr. Lionheart's testimony and cross-examination, Trust is visibly tense, seated at the defense table. His hands clasp so tightly they can break bones. His lips part like he wants to speak but thinks better of it. As Dr. Lionheart mentions the Cross and the nature of Trust, hope seems to soften his appearance. For a moment, the weight of the accusations lifts.

But when Reed presses, Trust deflates like a whoopie cushion. His gaze focuses only on the table. He dares not look up at the jury. Trust grapples with the enormity of the case, skeptical the jury can see beyond manipulation.

Shield breezes over to the defense table, picks up a tattered book, and motions to the judge. "Your Honor, the defense enters *Exhibit 7: The Writings of Flavius Josephus* into evidence. This critical piece of evidence supports the historical reality and impact of Jesus Christ. Josephus was a Jewish historian of the first century. He was neither a follower of Jesus nor was he writing as an advocate of the Christian faith. He was an observer of history, and his words are among the most compelling validations of the life and impact of Jesus of Nazareth."

The judge nods in agreement as the exhibit is so entered. The screen behind Shield glows, revealing Josephus's quotes.

Shield turns to the jury. "Josephus was born in AD 37, just a few years after Jesus's crucifixion. He was a Jewish religious leader, a Pharisee, and a military leader during the Jewish-Roman War. He later became an official historian for Rome under Emperor Vespasian. Josephus wrote extensively about the history of the Jewish people, and his works are regarded as some of the most reliable and comprehensive accounts of that time."

Shield gestures to the first passage.

"This passage is from Josephus's work, *Antiquities of the Jews*. Written around AD 93, it is known as the *Testimonium Flavianum*:

> 'Now there was about this time Jesus, a wise man, if it be lawful to call him a man, for he was a doer of wonderful works, a teacher of such men as receive the truth with pleasure. He drew over to him both many of the Jews and many of the Gentiles. He was [the] Christ; and when Pilate, at the suggestion of the principal men amongst us, had condemned him to the cross, those that loved him at the first did not forsake him; for he appeared to them alive again the third day, as the divine prophets had foretold these and ten thousand other wonderful things concerning him. And the

tribe of Christians, so named from him, are not extinct at this day."[7]

"Ladies and gentlemen, the author of these words is not a Christian apologist. They were penned by a historian whose intent was to document, not to persuade. Josephus describes Jesus as a historical figure, someone who existed, performed remarkable works, and inspired a following that persists to this very day."

Reed springs from his seat. "Objection! Your Honor, this passage has been the subject of scholarly debate for centuries. It is widely believed that Christian scribes may have altered Josephus's original text to make it more favorable to their cause."

The judge motions, throwing his hand forward at Shield, "Response, Counselor."

"Your Honor, we acknowledge that some scholars question the authenticity of certain phrases within this passage. However, the consensus is Josephus did indeed write about Jesus, even if later interpolations may have occurred. More importantly, there are other writings from Josephus that independently verify Jesus's existence and his impact."

The judge nods. "Very well. Proceed, but tread carefully."

"This section from Josephus provides yet another confirmation that Jesus was not a mythical figure but a real person whose influence extended to his family and followers."

Shield continues on. "Your Honor, the defense introduces *Exhibit 8: The Cross*. This symbol is not a religious artifact. It is a historical fact. Josephus was not the only historian to mention Jesus. Roman historians such as Tacitus and Suetonius also referenced Jesus' crucifixion under Pontius Pilate. What makes Josephus's account particularly striking is its close proximity to the events. He lived within a generation of Jesus' life and had access to firsthand witnesses.

"Josephus's writings confirm that Jesus' crucifixion was not a fabrication; it was a historical event. The Cross is a documented reality of ultimate Trust. And let's be honest, if anyone had a reason to say, 'I can't Trust God,' it was Jesus. He was betrayed, beaten, and crucified. And yet, what did he say? 'Father, not my will, but yours be done' (Luke 22:42). That's real Trust. Not Trust that avoids pain but Trust that endures through it. And here's the kicker." Shield leans on the evidence table.

7. (Josephus 1986)

"When humanity sinned and separated themselves from God's holy presence, God didn't just sit back and say, 'Well, that sucks. Good luck.' No. He provided a way out by sending Jesus Christ to willingly take the consequence of sin, death. So that we could be reconciled to God. The Cross is the ultimate evidence of God's trustworthiness. It shows us that while God does not promise to remove our suffering, He does promise to be with us in it and to use it for our good."

Shield walks to the defense table and picks up a worn deck of cards. "Your Honor, the defense introduces *Exhibit 9: The Game of War*." He fans the cards out in his hand and approaches the jury. "In this game, Trust is everything. You Trust that the cards will be dealt fairly and that the rules will be followed. But how often do players cheat, stack the deck, or manipulate the game? Trust isn't at fault; it is the players who abuse it.

"Isn't that exactly what humanity does with Trust? We twist him. We manipulate him. And then we blame him when things don't go our way. But Trust, like the cards, is innocent. And that is a fact."

Shield walks back to the defense table and places the cards on the table. Next, he pulls out a crisp dollar bill, delicately pinched between his fingers. "Your Honor, the defense moves to admit *Exhibit 10: The Dollar Bill*, our final piece of evidence." Shield raises the bill high, the phrase "*In God We Trust*" emblazoned in bold letters on the back.

The judge studies him for a moment. "So entered. Proceed, Counselor."

Shield strides toward the jury with his left hand in his pocket, holding the bill up in his right like a sacred relic. "This is not just a piece of paper. It's not just currency. This is a symbol, a declaration. This is a testament to the values this country was founded on. Four simple words . . . *In God We Trust*. Etched not just onto this dollar but into the very fabric of our nation's identity."

He stops, taking a long moment to examine the room. The gallery, restless moments earlier, is now enchanted, hanging on his every word.

"When our founding fathers fled persecution and tyranny, they didn't seek riches or glory or power. They sought freedom, a refuge where they could worship without fear, a land where Trust in God would guide their paths without oppression. As they laid the foundation of this great country, they engraved their faith into its very framework. '*In God We Trust*.'"

Shield paces down the jury box, holding the bill in front of the jury like a mirror. "But I ask you: when did we lose sight of this? When did we stop believing in the ideals that built this great country? When did Trust in God become a relic, tucked away and forgotten, instead of prominently displayed as the cornerstone of our future? Have we changed so fundamentally? Have we become so cynical, so distant, so jaded that we put Trust itself on trial?"

Shield turns to the defense table, defiantly pointing at the defendant. "The truth is, it's not Trust that's changed. It's us. Somewhere along the way, we've strayed. We lost our way. We placed our faith in fleeting, temporary things—things like power, like wealth, like convenience—instead of focusing on what is essential, eternal."

Shield places the dollar bill, the physical embodiment of a larger truth, on the evidence table. "This phrase used to mean something. It was a rallying cry, a reminder that Trust, true Trust, must be placed in something greater than ourselves. And here we are, putting Trust on trial, questioning its validity, its worth. This dollar teaches us a resounding truth. And it is that Trust, when placed where it belongs, in God, becomes unshakable. Immutable. A foundation stronger than any courtroom argument or worldly possession can hold. It's a truth so simple and so profound, we've engraved it on our very currency. So I ask you, members of the jury, will you allow yourselves to forget it?"

Shield takes a step back. Pausing, allowing the gravity of his arguments to settle over the courtroom. "Ladies and gentlemen, today, we have proven beyond a shadow of a doubt the innocence of Trust. We've shown you evidence of its profound necessity. Through our witnesses, you've heard that Trust is not the perpetrator of pain. It is the victim of humanity's misuse and misunderstanding."

Shield signals toward Trust. Trust's expression is soft, his eyes hopeful. "Trust has been framed by the very people and systems that have abused it. You've heard witness testimony of trusting God through the deepest trials brings purpose to our pain. They've explained the modern error of placing God in the dock rather than confronting our own sin. And the evidence proves that Trust, when rightly placed, is not just reliable but unshakable and transformational.

"Yes, there is pain in this world. Yes, there is betrayal. But these are not Trust's crimes, they are humanity's."

Shield walks back over and picks up the dollar bill once more, thrusting it forward, holding it for the jury to see the words: "*In God We Trust.*"

"This dollar bill is a symbol, a solemn reminder that Trust in God is woven into the fabric of this nation. Our founding fathers recognized that no government, no institution, no human could bear the weight of our ultimate Trust. That Trust belongs to God. The defense rests, Your Honor."

Judge Steele slams the gavel down, the force of the strike creating a burst of air that shakes the front of his robe. "The defense has rested its case. Closing arguments will begin tomorrow morning. Court is adjourned."

The jury exits with the immense burden in front of them pressing on their minds. Outside, the world marches on, intently watching the battle unfold within these walls. Tomorrow, the final showdown for the fate of Trust begins. Everything hangs in the balance.

CHAPTER 7

The Trust War

Closing Arguments

THE COURTROOM IS ON THE VERGE of a full-blown cardiac episode. Everyone is on edge, the monitors on their smart watches going off constantly. *Warning. Cardiac Arrest Imminent.* Every creak of a chair, every cough, every sniffle, every rustle of paper magnifies the importance of today. The jurors fidget in their seats, the gravity of their decision weighing them down like chains. They will be the architects of a verdict that will ripple far beyond these walls.

Today is the crescendo, a culmination of an epic trial fueled with fire and fury. The prosecution and defense are ready to deliver their final symphonies, each argument sharpened, designed to sway the hearts and minds of the jury.

The stakes are colossal. Lives, legacies, and the fate of Trust itself hang in the balance. Brace for final impact. This is the knockout round, and the fight can go either way on the scorecards. Can either side deliver a knockout?

Trust sits calmly at the defense table. Nearly a week's worth of drama has overloaded his senses. His shoulders sag like he's been holding cinder blocks up with his hands for days. Heavy-lidded eyes, rimmed with fatigue, blink slower now, struggling to maintain focus. A deep sigh escapes, as if even breathing requires effort. His fingers rub at his temples then drag down his face, like he's trying to wipe away the exhaustion. His face is a kaleidoscope of emotions: vulnerability, resilience, optimism, hope, even fear.

Nevertheless, Trust forces himself to maintain some form of composure. His entire persona screams, *"Just keep it together. One more day."*

"All rise!" the bailiff announces. Judge Steele, the ever-stoic conductor of this symphony, surveys the room. He raises his gavel and slams it down. "Ladies and gentlemen, we have reached the final phase of this trial: closing arguments. The prosecution may begin."

Reed confidently stands; his tailored black suit shines as he approaches the jury. He pauses, peering into the souls of every juror. A moment of silence stretches on like an eternity.

"Ladies and gentlemen of the jury, we stand here today to unmask a con artist, a villain, a master manipulator who has woven himself into the fabric of humanity, only to betray us when we least expect it. We have shown you the true nature of Trust. Trust is not what he claims to be. He sits here, pretending to be our ally, a cornerstone of relationships, a strong pillar. But I implore you to look closer. Look beyond the façade, and you will see the truth. Trust is a liar, the definition of a fraud, a danger to all who dare to rely upon it. Trust is a cunning deceiver who promises safety while leading us into disaster.

"You've heard the witness testimonies. You've shed tears and shaken your heads at the devastation left behind by the defendant. You've seen the mountain of evidence. And you've felt the personal sting of betrayal. Trust stands charged with two crimes: *fraud* and *breach of contract.* These crimes are the culmination of your pain, your tears, and your shattered expectations.

"We heard from victims, parents, employees, friends, distinguished scholars, and even Mr. Nash, who suffered immeasurable loss because they dared to believe in Trust's lies. Trust is the foundation of every human interaction, every hope, every belief. It's the invisible glue that holds relationships, systems, and faith together. And yet, what have we seen in this very courtroom?

"We've seen Trust operate in an untrustworthy manner. This trial has exposed him as a co-conspirator and perpetrator of the biggest Ponzi scheme in history. Billions were stolen and thousands of heartbroken families were taken advantage of. And Trust was there, offering false security and hope for the future. Trust failed to deliver. He broke the contract. He committed the fraud. He kept tricking us into believing his lies.

"We've seen a parent's desperate attempt to control the uncontrollable, born out of shattered Trust that left walls of isolation in its wake. We've seen a philosopher dissect the very nature of suffering, painting a grim picture of how evil and pain make the idea of a Trustworthy God tantamount to wishful thinking. And we've heard a grieving father, aA man whose cries to God were met with cruel silence.

"And then we heard from an atheist. His testimony cuts deeper than most because it challenged not just relationships or systems but the very concept of a Trustworthy deity. 'If God can be trusted,' he asked, 'then why does suffering exist? Why does evil persist? Why does he stay silent?' These questions, ladies and gentlemen, are not just rhetorical; they are indictments."

Reed paces. "We've also shown you tangible evidence of Trust's crimes. The Wall of Isolation. The Game of Uno, the blame game we play when Trust fails. The Broken Clock. The Prayer Journal. And finally, the Empty Chair. Each one tells the same story: that Trust, no matter where it's placed, is fragile, unreliable, and often devastating.

"The defense will argue that Trust isn't broken, that we've just misplaced Trust. They will tell you that Trust in God is different, that God works in mysterious ways, that his plans are greater than we can comprehend. But is that not just another way of saying, 'Trust him blindly when the evidence screams otherwise'? But let me ask you this: where was God when Susan built her walls? Where was God when Dr. Lecture wrestled with the reality of evil? Where was God when Robert begged for his daughter's life? And where was Trust in all of this? Right there alongside, taking you on a horrific and detrimental ride.

"But the most damning evidence of all is you—your own experiences with Trust's betrayal, your history with Trust issues and brokenness that stretches a lifetime. How many promises has Trust broken in your life? How many relationships has Trust shattered? How many nights have you lain awake, wondering why you Trusted someone who let you down?"

Reed's voice elevates sharply. "The defense has tried to paint Trust as a victim, an innocent bystander in humanity's failures. But let me remind you: a victim does not actively deceive. A victim does not promise stability and deliver disaster. A victim does not lead people astray, while secretly whispering false assurances.

"Trust is not the victim; you are! Trust is a liar, a fraud, and a danger to society. And now it's your turn to hold Trust accountable. By finding Trust guilty, you deliver justice. You send a message: No more lies. No more false promises. No more blind faith in something so inherently flawed. No more accepting the betrayal, pain, and heartbreak as risks. You can break the cycle of broken trust. You can take back control."

Reed paces in front of the jury. "The defense has spent this entire trial hammering home one point: Trust and God are inseparable. Fine. Let's talk about that."

He pauses. "If Trust is the foundation of all belief, all faith, then what happens when the foundation crumbles? The defense wants you to believe Trust isn't the problem. Rather, it's humanity's misuse of Trust that's to blame. But let's take that argument a step further. If God is as good, as powerful, as sovereign as they claim, then every betrayal, every heartbreak, every tragedy is something he could have stopped—but didn't. What kind of Trust asks a grieving father to believe while he buries his child? What kind of Trust demands faith while wars rage, disasters strike, and the innocent suffer? Is this the kind of Trust that deserves your faith? Or is this the ultimate betrayal? And since the defense insists you can't separate Trust from God, doesn't that mean Trust is guilty after all?"

Reed looks the jurors in the eyes. "You might ask yourself, 'If I can't trust people, if I can't trust systems, if I can't even trust God . . . then what's the point? What's left?'

"That's the exact question we want you to consider. Why should we Trust anyone or anything? Can you, in good conscience, find Trust anything but guilty? Guilty of fraud. Guilty of breach of contract. Guilty of leaving a trail of broken hearts, shattered dreams, and ruined lives in his path. The evidence speaks for itself. The victims cry out for justice. The truth is staring you right in the face. Trust has failed us. Isn't it safer to rely on ourselves? To build walls, take control, and avoid the pain of misplaced Trust? Isn't it better to live with the certainty that no one, will come through for you?"

The prosecutor walks slowly back to his table. "We rest our case, confident that the evidence speaks for itself. Will you continue to place your faith in something so dangerous, so unreliable? Or will you accept the truth that Trust, no matter where it's placed, is a risk too great to take? Thank you."

The prosecution rests. Reed sucks all the air out of the room, daring you to make sense of it all. What happens next is up to you.

The courtroom is on sensory overloaded. Every eye focuses on Shield as he stands one final time. Trust sits at the defense table. He squares his shoulders, straightens his spine, and lets out a calming exhale. He's got serious bags under his eyes. A rollercoaster of emotions, ranging from excitement to fear, courses through his veins. This is it. No more objections. No more exhibits. Just one last plea for the truth. Trust dares to believe this last hurrah will tip the scales in his favor. They call that . . . hope.

Shield adjusts his jacket, buttons the top button, and approaches the jury. "Ladies and gentlemen of the jury, a lot of accusations have been hurled at Trust throughout the course of this trial. I don't envy you one bit. Trust stands accused of *fraud* and *breach of contract*. The prosecution has called witnesses, presented exhibits, and spun a narrative that would have you believe Trust is a manipulative and deceitful liar, an evil villain lurking in the shadows of human relationships, a thief, a complicit co-conspirator, and a killer. But I ask you, does the evidence before you support that? Or is it simply an attempt to find a scapegoat for humanity's own failures?

"Look at the witnesses the prosecution presented. Greed caused men like Bernie Madoff to abuse Trust. Madoff's Ponzi scheme was not the result of Trust's failure. It was the result of deceit. Remember Mr. Jones, a grieving father who lost his daughter in her battle with cancer? Even though his Trust in God wavered, he still Trusted. He still believed in God and believed in heaven. He Trusted in a dream of a place where suffering and pain don't exist.

"Remember Ms. Payne who caught her husband cheating? Her life was wrecked. Her Trust was shattered—by her ex-husband. It wasn't Trust who had an affair. It wasn't Trust who lied and attempted to blame Ms. Payne. It wasn't Trust who went behind her back. Do you see the pattern? The betrayal of a friend is not a flaw in Trust; it is a flaw in the friend. The failure of institutions is not a sign that Trust is irredeemable; it is evidence that humanity is. We've blamed Trust for the hurt caused by broken promises, betrayed loved ones, and failing institutions. What is the common denominator in all these heartbreaking cases? Is it Trust? Or is it the people and systems that abused him?"

Shield points at Trust. "Look at the defendant. Look at the damage this trial has inflicted on Trust. Trust does not argue for itself. It does not plead for sympathy. Why? Because Trust knows its own nature. It knows it is innocent. Trust is not the criminal here. Trust is the victim. A victim of misplaced faith, false expectations, and deliberate sabotage. A victim of the enemy's deliberate schemes that would have you focus on Trust rather than believe in his existence.

"Are we so short-sighted we forget who the real culprits are? Trust has been framed by broken, flawed, and self-serving humans. Framed by humanity's unwillingness to confront its own sin. Framed by an adversary who seeks to deceive, kill, and destroy. Framed by a world that demands guarantees yet offers none in return. So, I ask you: Can you really convict Trust when the real culprit has been staring back at you in the mirror?"

Shield hesitates, allowing the jury to contemplate. "Ladies and gentlemen, the fault does not lie with Trust. The fault lies with us. We ask Trust to hold the weight of the world, but we sabotage its foundation. We place it in fragile things—failing people, corrupt systems, fleeting promises—and then cry foul when it collapses."

Shield inches closer to the jury, softening his voice. "The defense presented witnesses who testified to triumph when their Trust was rightly placed. Through Mr. Harrison, we saw that Trust in God can endure through the greatest moments of suffering. Through Dr. Abrams, we offered historical accounts of Abraham and the faithfulness of a God who provides. Through the three college students, we were reminded that even in the fiery furnace of life's trials, Trust in God is unshakable.

"Remember Staff Sergeant Mercer who testified about the realities of facing a giant? Not some metaphor, not just an impossible situation but a living, breathing nightmare. He was trapped behind enemy lines, outgunned, outnumbered, and staring certain death in the face. And what did he have? No backup. No heavy artillery. No tactical advantage. He wasn't *John Wick* incarnate. All he had was his training, his instinct, and his Trust. It would've been easy to give up. To surrender and let fear take over. But Mercer did what David did. He faced the impossible. And like David who faced Goliath, armed with five smooth stones and unshakeable faith, Mercer stood his ground. He believed, even in the valley of the shadow of death, that he wasn't alone.

"David looked at Goliath and said, 'You come at me with sword and spear, but I come at you in the name of the Lord Almighty' (1 Samuel 17:45). And what happened? That giant fell. Just like Staff Sergeant Mercer, who overcame impossible odds and made it back home from the battlefield. And let's be clear: David and Goliath isn't some fairytale. Archaeological evidence from the ruins of Gath proves that Goliath's hometown actually existed. It confirms David's Trust. David didn't win because of brute force, superior weapons, or sheer luck. He won because he placed his Trust in something greater.

"And that is what this case is really about. Because if Trust can carry us through the impossible, if it can bring a soldier back from certain death, then ask yourselves . . . where would we be without Trust?

"Dr. Lionheart challenged us to confront the reality of our own hearts, to examine our beliefs and our actions. He warned us that humanity has reversed the roles, placing God in the dock and ourselves on the bench. But as Dr. Lionheart stated, there are only three possibilities when it comes to Jesus Christ: he is either a liar, a lunatic, or he is Lord. The Cross stands as the ultimate evidence of his lordship. The prosecution would have you believe that God cannot be Trusted because suffering exists. But the Cross tells a different story—a story of redemption, a historical fact, corroborated by witnesses like Josephus, the Jewish historian. He recorded the life, death, and enduring impact of Jesus Christ. The Cross is the most profound act of Trustworthiness in history: a God who entered into our suffering to provide a way out of it. It is the evidence of a God who is with us, who loves us, and who is Trustworthy beyond measure."

Shield turns, gesturing toward Reed. "The prosecution has pulled out all the stops in their case against Trust, haven't they? Yet, even in their arguments, they have unwittingly acknowledged its power. They argue Trust is too fragile, unreliable, and invaluable. Every witness they called, every exhibit they presented relies on Trust to carry its weight. The prosecution has placed its Trust in the jury's ability to discern the truth from the witnesses and the integrity of the evidence. Do you see the irony? Even as they condemn Trust, they depend on him.

"If Trust were irredeemable, would we even be having this trial? Would the prosecution have pursued this case? No, ladies and gentlemen, not at all. This trial exists because Trust matters. Because, even in our brokenness, we cannot escape the reality that Trust is essential to our existence."

Shield paces, then walks over to the defense table. He pulls out a dollar bill. He looks at the bill, turning it toward the jury and carefully walking it in front of each juror, letting them take in the familiar green and white, tapping his finger on the bold words printed on the back: "In God We Trust."

"Ladies and gentlemen, this isn't just a piece of paper. It's a message, a cornerstone of our nation's true identity. This phrase," he says, tapping the words again, "has been carried in wallets, passed across counters, folded into church offering plates, and tossed into fountains with the hopes of a wish. It's traveled through time, connecting generations with a simple truth: Trust is a declaration of faith.

"When our nation's founders crafted the framework for this country, they didn't do so lightly. They fled persecution, leaving behind tyranny and oppression, seeking a place where freedom—true freedom—could flourish. Our founders believed in something greater than themselves. It guided their actions and gave them hope. Those beliefs weren't whispers in the shadows. They were carved into the very foundations of this country, engraved into its symbols. Our framers left a lasting legacy and their convictions endure. Right here," he raises the bill slightly higher.

"But what about us? What have we done with that Trust? Somewhere along the way, we stopped believing. We stopped living the ideals this phrase represents. 'In God We Trust.' A bold declaration, but I ask you now: how many of us still live by these words? How many of us truly consider what it means? Why have so many abandoned it for something else?"

Shield pauses, his voice dropping to a whisper. "This dollar is fragile. It's a flimsy piece of paper, easy to crumple, easy to tear and toss aside. But what about the Trust it represents? This case isn't just about Trust as a defendant. It's about Trust as a foundation, a way of life. And I submit that the problem isn't Trust. The problem is us. We've grown skeptical, distrustful, cynical. What happens to a nation that forgets the foundation it was built upon? What happens when it abandons the very ideals that gave it life?"

Shield places the dollar bill on the juror's box. "This simple piece of paper is a challenge, a call to remember what matters most: to place our Trust in something greater, something eternal. Because without Trust, everything else falls apart."

Shield takes one final step back. "Ladies and gentlemen, the fate of Trust rests in your hands."

Trust sits quietly, tears filling his eyes from the fiery defense. As Shield makes his final plea, you can feel Trust saying, "*Just give me a chance.*"

"I ask you to look beyond the surface of this trial. Look beyond the accusations and the pain. Look beyond your doubts and your fears. Ask yourself: Is Trust guilty or has humanity failed to use it correctly? If you condemn Trust today, you aren't rendering a verdict on an idea. You render a verdict on your own heart, on your own capacity to believe, to hope, to love. Ladies and gentlemen, I implore you. Do not condemn Trust for humanity's sins. Set it free. And in doing so, set yourselves free. I ask you to render the only verdict that makes sense. Declare Trust NOT GUILTY, and in doing so, give humanity the chance to rebuild, to heal, to forgive, and ultimately, to hope. Allow me to ask you this . . . what kind of world exists without Trust?"

He stops, takes a deep breath, and lets the question hang. "A world without Trust is a world where love cannot thrive, where relationships crumble, where promises hold no meaning, and where fear dictates every decision. Is that the world you want to live in? Because that is the verdict the prosecution asks you to deliver. A world where no one dares to believe, to hope, to risk. A world dictated by fear. A world where trust dies and suspicion reigns supreme. The prosecution demands you convict Trust, that you declare him guilty. And if that's the case, then I have one final question for you . . ."

He inches closer, ". . . Why should you trust them?"

The echo of his final words lingers as Shield returns his seat. As Shield delivers his final argument, Reed stares at the jury, questioning the certainties of his case. Is Trust guilty or innocent?

CHAPTER 8

Jury Deliberations

THE COURTROOM IS QUIET, eerily so. All eyes turn to Judge Steele. His gavel, a simple wooden mallet, lays still but armed with authority, a reminder that the next words will chart the course for Trust's fate.

Judge Steele adjusts his glasses and clears his throat. "Ladies and gentlemen of the jury, you have heard the arguments. You have seen the evidence. And now, the burden of rendering a verdict falls squarely upon your shoulders. This is not an ordinary trial, and the defendant is no ordinary figure. Trust sits before you, accused of fraud and breach of contract.

"To convict Trust of *fraud*, you must conclude that the prosecution has proven beyond a reasonable doubt that Trust knowingly deceived and misled humanit, luring people into situations where betrayal and pain were inevitable. The question is simple: did Trust actively participate in this deceit, or was it merely manipulated by those who wield it?"

The judge pauses, scanning the faces of the jury, taking a pulse of the courtroom. "To convict Trust of *breach of contract*, you must conclude that Trust failed to uphold an implicit agreement with humanity, an agreement that Trust would lead to certainty, security, and reliability. The prosecution argues that Trust has consistently failed to deliver on these promises, leaving behind a trail of broken relationships, shattered dreams, and unmet expectations.

"Remember, jurors, your decision will have consequences far beyond this courtroom. Trust has been placed on trial, not just for his actions but for his very existence. A verdict of guilty would condemn him as a dangerous individual unworthy of reliance, while a verdict of not guilty would vindicate him as a misunderstood victim of human failure.

"The jury will now deliberate. The fate of Trust lies in your hands. You may retire to the jury deliberation room."

WHAM!

Judge Steele's gavel cracks through the courtroom, and the jury stands in unison. An anxious, crowded gallery watches them eagerly as they file out, a heavy sense of responsibility weighing on their sagging shoulders.

The courtroom has emptied. All eyes fixate on the deliberations unfolding behind the jury room's closed doors.

Down the hall in a quiet conference room, another conflict is mounting. Reed sits at the table. The lines around his eyes are deeper, his tie loosened just a smidge. Across from him, Shield leans back in his chair, his jacket unbuttoned and his chin turned up at Reed. To the left of Shield sits Trust—calm, his arms crossed and resting on his belly as if to say, "*I'm ready for whatever happens next.*"

Reed clears his throat, breaking the uncomfortable silence. "You know, Shield, I've been doing this a long time. I've seen a lot of cases. Some slam dunks, some nail-biters. This one? It's not what I thought it would be."

Shield arches his eyebrow but remains quiet.

"Your closing argument? I'll admit, it was solid. Good, maybe even great. You've got the jury thinking, and that's a dangerous thing." Reed slowly glances over at Trust, his beady eyes narrowing. "But let's not kid ourselves. This could go either way. And if the jury swings my way? Trust loses everything.

"So, here's the deal. Seven years. Parole in three and a half for good behavior. No more uncertainty, no more risking it all on the whims of twelve strangers. You live to fight another day. It's not perfect, but it's a hell of a lot better than what's waiting for you on the other side if you lose."

Shield leans forward slightly, his hands clasped together. For a moment, the room holds its breath. Shield turns to Trust. "What do you think? It's your life on the line here. Not mine. Take a moment and weigh everything before you answer."

Trust meets Shield's gaze. He answers with a slow, defiant head shake.

Shield's lips curl into a faint smile. "Well, there you have it." He rocks back and forth in his chair. "No deal. We'll take our chances."

Reed tightens his jaw, his lips barely moving. "You're making a mistake, Shield. A big one."

"Maybe," Shield stands, sliding his hands into his pockets. "But that's for the jury to decide now, isn't it?" He winks at Reed while his mouth is half open on one side. "Thanks for the offer though, big guy. Really."

Reed stays seated as Trust and Shield exit the room. He whispers, "Idiots."

The jury deliberation room isn't a sterile, fluorescent-lit picture of perfection as you might expect. No, they built this place for contemplation. The polished light-wooden table in the center of the room bears the scars of decades of deliberations, etched with faint scratches and the occasional chip. Around the table sit twelve chairs, angled slightly inward, intentionally placed for inviting dialogue.

Corkboards and whiteboards adorn the walls, each section meticulously divided between the prosecution and the defense. The evidence, pinned and labeled, challenges the jurors to engage. There is *Exhibit A: The Apple of Eden*, sitting in a protective case on a side table. Its gleaming surface taunting in its simplicity. Next to it rests *Exhibit B: The Bag of Silver Coins*. The metallic clinking still echoes in their memory.

The defense exhibits stand in defiance. A worn Bible rests on a wooden stand, its pages bookmarked to the stories of Abraham, Job, David, and Shadrach, Meshach, and Abed-Nego. Nearby is a photo of the Foundation Stone. Its jagged edges are a stark contrast to the prosecution's polished symbols. A smaller section of the room displays photographs of archaeological finds such as Nebuchadnezzar's kiln bricks, the Babylonian furnaces, and fragments of the city of Gath. Each serves as a silent witness to the defense.

A stack of legal pads and pens sits in the center of the table, inviting the jurors to write their thoughts or maybe even jot down their doubts.

Questions hang heavy in the air as the jury members find their seats. Only the sound of creaking chairs and rustling papers fills the room. Each noise is a small reminder of the monumental decision in front of them.

The foreperson, an older woman in her early sixties with curly white hair, stands and reads aloud from a laminated sheet labeled "Prosecution Summary."

"The prosecution has made the following arguments:

1. *The Charges*

- Fraud: Trust lures humanity into false security and confidence, knowing it cannot deliver.

- Breach of Contract: Trust fails to uphold its implicit promise to provide certainty, reliability, and safety.

2. *Witness Testimonies*

- The Madoff Victim: Trust co-conspired in a billion-dollar Ponzi scheme, enabling financial devastation and the loss of life savings.
- The Business Owner: Trust betrayed them by using their business partner and their belief in stability, leading to bankruptcy and the collapse of a lifelong dream.
- The Betrayed Child: Trust failed to protect and fulfill, leaving deep emotional scars and a lifetime of self-blame.
- The Disillusioned Employee: Highlighted institutional failures as evidence of Trust's systemic unreliability.
- The Heartbroken Partner: Trust enabled infidelity, leaving emotional wreckage and a broken foundation of love.
- The Overbearing Parent: Trust's failure caused a spiral of control, anxiety, and damaged relationships.
- The Skeptical Philosopher: Argued that Trust is fundamentally flawed. Trusting in a good God is contradictory to the existence of evil, suffering, and death.
- The Brokenhearted Parent: Trust breached their own contract, failing to deliver answers in the face of unanswered prayers and unbearable grief.
- The Atheist: Reasoned Trust in God is not only misplaced; it's delusional. Offering false hope in a broken universe. Points to suffering as proof of God's untrustworthiness.

3. *Exhibits*

- Exhibit A: The Apple of Eden, symbolizing humanity's first betrayal of Trust.
- Exhibit B: The Bag of Silver Coins, demonstrating how Trust can lead to ultimate betrayal.
- Exhibit C: The Hall of Broken Trust, illustrating Trust's failures throughout history.

- Exhibit D: The Bernie Madoff Ponzi Scheme, one of the most heinous cases of fraud in history. Resulted in billions of dollars stolen and the exploitation of Trust itself. His victims believed in him, in the institutions he represented, and in the promises he made.

- Exhibit E: A Broken Business Contract, a symbol of every promise ever broken. This contract represents a business deal gone wrong and costs a small-town entrepreneur his livelihood.

- Exhibit F: The Game of Uno, a depiction of the cyclical and chaotic nature of the blame game.

- Exhibit G: A Broken Doll, a symbol of childhood Trust shattered.

- Exhibit H: A Severance Notice, an impersonal document that represents the betrayal of Trust in institutions.

- Exhibit I: A Torn Wedding Photo, a visceral reminder of how infidelity shatters Trust.

- Exhibit J: The Wall of Isolation, representing the barriers we build to protect ourselves when Trust fails.

- Exhibit K: The Broken Clock, symbolizing humanity's futile attempts to control time, outcomes, and circumstances when Trust fails.

- Exhibit L: The Prayer Journal, representing a cry for help, a plea for intervention. Each unanswered prayer is a testament to Trust's failure.

- Exhibit M: The Empty Chair, symbolizing every unanswered prayer, every moment of divine silence, every time someone cried out to God and received silence.

4. *Core Argument*

- The prosecution argued Trust is fundamentally unreliable, complicit in every betrayal, heartbreak, systemic and institutional failure. Across personal, institutional, and divine relationships, Trust has proven dangerous, manipulative, irredeemable, and unworthy of belief.

- Seeking a guilty verdict on one count of fraud and one count of breach of contract, leaving a trail of devastation that demands accountability and damages."

The foreperson nonchalantly places the stapled sheets down on the table. She then picks up the corresponding sheet labeled "Defense Summary."

"The defense has argued the following points:

1. *Core Argument*

- Trust is not the problem. Trust, like everyone in the courtroom, is a victim. The problem doesn't lie with Trust but in where and how humanity places their Trust. Misplaced Trust leads to pain, but rightly placed Trust in the Most High God is transformational.

2. *Witness Testimonies*

- Dr. Gideon Abrams: The historian and archeologist showed Abraham's unwavering Trust in God despite overwhelming odds.

- Staff Sergeant Daniel Mercer: The soldier trapped behind enemy lines faced his own version of Goliath. His testimony showed that Trust in God can triumph over insurmountable challenges.

- The Three College Students: They provided an example of Trust in the face of the fiery trials of life.

- James Harrison: He endured unimaginable suffering and loss during a Category Five hurricane. Yet, he didn't abandon his Trust in God. Because of his faith and Trust, God blessed him twice as much as he lost.

- Dr. Malcolm Lionheart: The renowned philosopher and former atheist offered a philosophical perspective, framing humanity's issue as one of misplaced blame and failure to recognize sin.

3. *Exhibits*

- Exhibit 1: The Bible, a historical record of Trustworthiness.

- Exhibit 2: The Foundation Stone, tangible evidence of Abraham's story.

- Exhibit 3: God's Attributes, an outline of the characteristics of God that prove his trustworthiness.

- Exhibit 4: The Account of David and Goliath, the historical record of Trust in action, overcoming impossible odds.

- Exhibit 4: Artifacts of Gath and the Philistines, showcasing archeological findings of the ancient city of Gath, the confirmed home of Goliath, and artifacts that prove the historical reality of the Philistines.

- Exhibit 6: Babylonian Artifacts, including kiln-fired bricks inscribed with King Nebuchadnezzar's name and records of Babylonian furnace construction, corroborating the historical and cultural setting described in Daniel's account.

- Exhibit 7: The Writings of Flavius Josephus, corroborating the existence and significance of Jesus Christ as a historical figure.

- Exhibit 8: The Cross, the ultimate symbol of sacrifice and divine Trustworthiness.

- Exhibit 9: The Game of War, explaining the game of chance humans play to twist, manipulate, and blame when things go wrong. But Trust, like the cards, is innocent.

- Exhibit 10: The Dollar Bill, not just currency but a symbol. It stands as a testament to the values this country was built on. Four simple words, "In God We Trust," etched onto the dollar and the very fabric of our nation's identity.

4. *Rebuttals to Prosecution*

- Trust is a victim not a villain. He has been manipulated and abused. And he stands falsely accused.

- Offered two alternate suspects. 1. The devil: a master of deception who manipulates humanity and twists their perceptions of Trust and God to hide his evil. 2. Humanity: they misuse and take advantage of Trust for their own personal gain. Suffering and betrayal are results of sin and human error, not Trust itself.

- Seeking a verdict of not guilty. Argued Trust is a victim of humanity's misuse and misunderstanding. Trust is unshakable, life-changing, and the answer to the very pain and suffering the prosecution highlights when rightly placed in God."

The foreperson lays the sheets down, a faint wrinkling in her brow as she looks around the room at the jurors.

As the jury begins deliberations, they will sort through the evidence, debate the testimonies, and weigh the evidence. For every point the prosecution raises, the defense offers a counterpoint. And now, the decision rests with you.

Is Trust guilty of fraud and breach of contract? Or was Trust framed—a mere pawn, a patsy, a victim of humanity's misuse and the devil's deception?

An officer of the court leads Trust away to the confines of a small holding room adjacent to the courtroom. He sits alone, isolated. The fluorescent lights overhead cast shadows across the walls. The walls are bare, gray, lifeless—another box meant to contain him. He slumps slightly, hands clasped tightly in his lap.

Trust closes his eyes. He exhales slowly. His thoughts are a tornado. The faces of the jurors flash in his mind. Their expressions are still visible in his mind. Every question asked, every piece of evidence presented replays like a black-and-white film. Was it enough?

He squeezes his eyes, but the images keep pouring in.

- The prosecutor's booming accusations.

- The prosecution's evidence, cold and calculating, twists like a knife against his rigid spin.

- Judge Steele's solemn stare, impartial yet crushing.

And then, the defense. His lawyer, Harvey Shield. His steady presence. His assuring voice. Shield believed in him. He gave everything to fight for him. But will it be enough to undo every accusation tossed at him like a live grenade?

Earnest Trust, shaky and sincere, raises his head and lifts his eyes toward the ceiling. He begins to whisper, "If there's a chance for them to see me for what I truly am, let it happen now. But if this is the end, Lord, give me the strength to bear it."

Trust leans back, his head resting against the icy wall, staring into the emptiness. The excruciating weight of the trial and the impending verdict presses down on him. The silence stretches on.

But then. A sound.

A faint, distant shuffle. Then the distinct *CLICK* of a lock disengaging. Trust holds his breath.

The doorknob turns, slowly. The groaning hinges fill Trust with a mixture of expectation, fear, anxiety, and something more.

A shadowy figure blocks the doorway, lit up by the hall lights. For a split second, there's nothing. No words. Just the heaviness of what comes next.

And then . . . "It's time."

Your Decision Determines the Outcome

- *If Trust is Guilty*, proceed to Chapter 9.
- If Trust is Not Guilty, proceed to Chapter 10.

  Cast Your Verdict Now: https://gsgerry.com/books/trust-on-trial

CHAPTER 9

Guilty Verdict

THIS IS IT! The moment we've all been waiting for. Everyone is on the edge of their seats as our journey reaches its epic conclusion.

Trust looks like he hasn't slept a wink. His swollen eyes are barely open; he looks like a boxer who's taken a beating. This trial pushed him to his breaking point. His head hangs low. He scans the courtroom. No matter which way the verdict swings, Earnest Trust accepts his fate. His suit is a hot mess, constantly changing through the trial, now showing signs of fraying. His hands won't stop fidgeting. His cufflinks rattle against the defense table. It's impossible to hide the nerves pouring out of him.

Every seat is occupied. The gallery, overflowing with onlookers, leans forward. It's standing room only as everyone in the courtroom is sitting on pins and needles. It's dead silent except for the quiet *click-click* of cameras in the room. The still shots immortalize the stress on everyone's faces.

The clock's rhythmic ticking echoes through the stillness, measuring out the seconds until the jury foreperson rises. All eyes follow the foreperson as the jury files in. Her movements seemed to pause time itself. Judge Steele's gavel rests, poised. One final question will determine the fate of Trust.

Judge Steele's steady voice slices through the silence, "Ladies and gentlemen of the jury, have you reached a verdict?"

"We have, Your Honor," The foreperson's voice is firm as she passes the verdict to the bailiff.

Judge Steele quickly scans the verdict and hands it back. "Very well. Would the defendant please rise? Members of the jury, what say you?"

The foreperson swallows hard, the lump in her throat moving up and down like an accordion. She clears her throat. "On the charges of *fraud* and *breach of contract*, we find the defendant, Trust, *G-U-I-L-T-Y* on all counts."

The courtroom erupts! *GASPS!* of disbelief, betrayal, and vindication overtake the courtroom. Shield glances at his client. Trust doesn't move. He just stares off into the distance. His vibrant energy from the trial's opening days is now fully extinguished. Trust finally snaps out of his stoic expression and displays all the human emotions. His hands clutch the edge of the table, holding himself up from dropping to the floor in agony. He drops his head, shaking it back and forth. He is the scapegoat for humanity's blame. Trust is convicted on all counts of crimes he cannot fully comprehend.

Triumph, anger, sorrow, and regret are on full display on the gallery's faces. A mother clutches her young daughter, whispering, "Justice has been served." An elderly man removes his hat, as if in mourning over the loss of something vital.

Reed, meanwhile, has a victorious smirk splattered across his face. He scans the courtroom, pumping his fist, eagerly awaiting the moment to bask in triumph.

Judge Steele turns to the defendant. "Earnest Trust, you have been found guilty of *fraud* and *breach of contract*. The court will now impose a sentence that reflects the magnitude of your crimes."

Everyone braces for impact.

"Your actions have resulted in incalculable harm: broken hearts, shattered lives, and fractured faith spanning a lifetime. The prosecution argued convincingly for damages on a grand scale that accounts for the magnitude of your impact on humanity."

Judge Steele pauses, flipping through his notes. "For financial restitution, the court orders damages in the amount of $1,000 *per individual on Earth, multiplied by the current global population of eight billion people.* This totals $8 trillion, a sum that will be distributed equally to every man, woman, and child."

The enormity of the financial penalty is unprecedented, a figure so large it defies comprehension.

"As for incarceration, the court sentences you to indefinite confinement. You will remain under lock and key, prohibited from engaging with humanity until such a time as a higher court sees fit to overturn this decision. Until then, you remain a cautionary tale, a symbol of humanity's reckoning with its own failures. This sentence reflects the court's belief that you are no longer safe in the fabric of human relationships."

Trust places his head in his hands, a defeated figure whose once-proud aura has dissolved. His face shows the full impact of the verdict.

Shield leans over, his voice trembling as he whispers, "I'm so sorry. We gave it everything we had."

Trust finally raises his head, looking at the jury with a haunting, unspoken disbelief, questioning, "*Was it truly me? Or was it you all along?*"

Judge Steele slams the gavel, the sound tolling like a funeral bell. "Court is adjourned." The trial of the century has reached its dramatic conclusion.

Outside the courthouse, a sea of reporters floods the courthouse steps, waiting for Reed to bound through the doors. Microphones jut out from every angle as Reed confidently steps to the podium. A slow, creeping smirk tugs at the corner of his mouth. His eyes gleam, soaking in the moment like warm sunshine. His chin lifts, the kind of quiet arrogance that doesn't need words, just the subtle rise of his brows. There's a measured exhale through his nose that echoes in the microphone. Reed savors a victory he saw coming all along. He carries a mixture of triumph and something else—a shadow of doubt, perhaps?

"Ladies and gentlemen, today, justice has been served. For too long, Trust has operated without accountability, leaving a trail of heartbreak, betrayal, and shattered lives in its wake. This trial was not about punishment or retribution; it was about closure. It was about giving humanity the vindication it deserves. It means that we will no longer accept blind reliance. We will question, we will verify, and we demand that Trust be earned, not assumed.

"This verdict sends a clear message: no one is above the law. Trust has finally been held accountable for the pain it has enabled across humanity."

Applause roars from the courthouse steps, reverberating off the courthouse pillars.

Reed raises a hand, demanding silence. "This verdict is not a condemnation of hope or faith. It is a recognition that Trust is dangerous. It invites pain. It invites betrayal. And today, we say, 'Enough is enough.'"

Reed hesitates for a fraction of a second. "And yet, I must admit, the defense made several compelling arguments. As I listened to the final questions from Mr. Shield imploring us to consider a world absent of Trust, I did some soul-searching. Their plea to place Trust rightly—in God—resonated, even with me.

"I wholeheartedly stand with the jury's decision, but I cannot ignore the lingering question: If Trust is truly the victim of humanity's actions, then where does the real fault lie? Is it with us? Is it with something else, someone else? This is a bittersweet victory, and these questions will haunt me, and perhaps they should haunt us all. Thank you, that's all for now."

Reed leaves the podium amidst a flurry of questions.

Moments later, Defense Attorney Shield approaches the podium. His expression is solemn. "Today's verdict is a historical moment. It sets a precedent not just for Trust but for how we as a society approach accountability and blame." Shields gestures to the courthouse. "We've opened Pandora's Box; expect an enormous wave of similar cases to follow. If Trust can be tried and convicted, what stops us from putting Hope on trial for false promises? What prevents us from convicting Faith for misguided belief? Will we someday see Love accused of emotional harm and heartbreak? This verdict invites a dangerous precedent. We must proceed cautiously down this slippery slope.

"But despite the legal implications, let's not forget what this trial revealed. While Trust was convicted, he is not the villain here. Trust has been misused, abused, and scapegoated for humanity's flaws. If we continue to externalize blame instead of looking inward, we risk not only losing Trust but everything it holds together—relationships, community, forgiveness, and even faith."

He pauses, his voice dropping to a whisper. "We urge everyone to reflect on this verdict, not as a victory or a loss, but as a mirror. What does it say about us that we would rather blame Trust than confront our own shortcomings? Blaming Trust is easy. Taking responsibility for our actions is not."

A reporter shouts from the crowd, "What's next for Trust?"

"Trust will face indefinite confinement." Shield sighs, looking down at the podium, his eyebrows pinched and his nose wrinkling. "But I refuse to believe this is the end. Appeals will be filed, and higher courts, whether earthly or divine, will revisit this case. Until then, I urge the people to consider where you place your Trust. Is it in flawed people, systems, or things? Or is it in something unshakable?"

With that, Shield steps away, leaving the crowd to contemplate and the world to grapple with the verdict.

The Internet erupts moments after the verdict is announced. The seismic decision of Trust's guilt sends shockwaves across social media. Memes, think pieces, and heated debates flood timelines with hashtags sparking global conversations about the implications of the case.

For many, the ruling validates their deep-seated fears about vulnerability and connection. "*#TrustIsGuilty* confirms what I've always known," one user writes. "Trust is a scam, and I'm done with it."

Others reflect on their personal heartbreaks, sharing stories of betrayal under trending tags. A flood of short videos appears under hashtags like *#BrokenPromises* and *#NoMoreTrust* with users tearing up wedding vows, shredding contracts, and dramatically deleting contact lists.

1. *#TrustIsGuilty*: The top trending tag worldwide, used by supporters to express anger, cynicism, and despair over broken trust.

2. *#TrustOnTrial*: A catchall hashtag used to chronicle the trial from start to finish, littered with debates and reactions to the ruling.

3. *#BrokenPromises*: A hashtag used to share personal stories of betrayal and heartbreak, tied to the prosecution's case.

4. *#NoMoreTrust*: A rallying cry for those who believe the jury's verdict was the start of a new, guarded era.

5. *#TheEndOfTrust*: A dramatic hashtag capturing the sentiment of the ruling as the death knell for human connection.

6. *#JusticeForTheBroken*: A tag championing the jury's decision as justice for victims of misplaced trust.

But the backlash is not universal. Counter-movements emerge, with skeptics questioning the jury's decision. "If Trust is guilty, what hope do any of us have left?" one tweet asks, garnering thousands of retweets and likes with the hashtag *#TrustInShambles*.

The courthouse steps are a media frenzy as reporters scramble to capture reactions to the guilty verdict in the historic trial of The People v. Trust. Amidst the camera clicks and hurried questions, Juror Three, a stoic man in his late forties, agrees to sit down for an exclusive interview.

Juror Three prepares to explain the verdict that shocked the world.

Reporter: "Thank you for speaking with us today. This trial has gripped the nation and the world, and the verdict has already sparked fierce debate. What led the jury to declare Trust guilty of fraud and breach of contract?"

Juror Three: [Exhaling deeply] "It was an agonizing decision; one we didn't take lightly. But when we laid out all the evidence, the pattern became impossible to ignore. Trust isn't the innocent bystander the defense tried to portray it as. It's the root cause of so much of the pain and betrayal we've seen throughout history. It felt like the evidence demanded accountability."

Reporter: "Let's start with the prosecution's case. What evidence or testimony stood out to you the most?"

Juror Three: "There were so many compelling moments. But if I had to choose one, it was the testimonies from the victims. They painted a devastating picture of the carnage left behind by broken Trust. The Bernie Madoff victim was unforgettable. She described losing her entire life savings because she Trusted a man who turned out to be a predator. She even said, 'It wasn't just Madoff who betrayed me, it was Trust. I thought I could rely on it, but I was wrong.' That hit hard.

"And then there was the heartbroken partner who spoke about infidelity. The way she described the devastation of how that betrayal left her doubting everyone and everything, haunted me. It made me realize how fragile Trust really is.

"The business owner also stuck with me. He put his faith in partnerships and promises, only to watch his entire livelihood crumble. He said, 'Trust didn't just fail me; it destroyed me.' That was powerful."

Reporter: "Was there a specific piece of evidence that solidified your vote for guilt?"

Juror Three: "The prosecution's timeline of Trust's failures was damning. From the Garden of Eden to modern-day scandals like Ponzi schemes, it was clear that Trust has been complicit for centuries. And when they introduced the severance letter as evidence of institutional betrayal, it drove the point home. Trust isn't just fragile, it's guilty."

Reporter: "What about the defense's case? They made some strong points about humanity's misuse of Trust. Did their argument sway you at all?"

Juror Three: [Pausing, tapping his finger on his cheek.] "The defense gave a passionate argument, no doubt about it. They wanted us to believe that Trust is a victim, something pure that's been misused by humanity. They brought in powerful witnesses and historical evidence like Josephus's writings. Their presentation of 'In God We Trust' really left me reflecting. Those were compelling moments, but they didn't absolve Trust in my eyes. If anything, they made me more skeptical.

"For example, the Cross was presented as the ultimate evidence of trustworthiness. And while I respect the religious perspective, it didn't erase the fact that millions of people suffer because they placed their Trust in the wrong people or systems. Trust was still the common denominator."

Reporter: "What about Dr. Lionheart's testimony? He famously argued that Jesus is either a lunatic, a liar, or Lord. Did that resonate with you?"

Juror Three: [Nods] "It was a thought-provoking point. Dr. Lionheart was brilliant, no doubt about it. But here's the thing: Even if Jesus is Lord, that doesn't absolve Trust. The prosecution argued that Trust is like a loaded weapon. It can be used for good, but more often than not, it causes harm. That stuck with me."

Reporter: "Can you walk me through the deliberations?"

Juror Three: "The deliberations were intense. Some jurors were on the fence for a long time, and there were moments when I thought we might end up with a hung jury. But when we revisited the testimonies, we couldn't let Trust off the hook. We kept coming back to the same question: Can Trust really be separated from the pain it causes? The defense wanted us to believe that Trust is innocent, but the prosecution proved that Trust is the common thread in every betrayal, every failure, every heartbreak.

"One juror said, 'Trust's been complicit in too many crimes. It's impossible to ignore.' That sentiment resonated deeply with us all."

Reporter: "What do you think the guilty verdict means for society?"

Juror Three: [Sighing] "It's a wake-up call. We've been too quick to place blind Trust in people, institutions, and even ideas. This trial forced us to confront the consequences of that. I think the verdict sends a message: Trust needs to be earned, not freely given away. And we, as a society, need to be more discerning about where we place it. Otherwise, we're just setting ourselves up for more pain."

Reporter: "Do you think this verdict will change how people approach Trust?"

Juror Three: [Nods] "I hope so. If nothing else, people will be more cautious. I think this trial showed us the importance of accountability."

Reporter: "One final question: How has this trial changed your own perspective on Trust?"

Juror Three: "It's made me more careful, that's for sure. I used to think of Trust as something sacred, something unbreakable. But now I see it differently. Trust is fragile, and it needs to be handled with care. That doesn't mean I'll stop Trusting altogether. But it does mean I'll think twice before I hand over my Trust to someone, or something, again. And I hope others will do the same."

Juror Three's words carry a sobering reality, a reflection of the trial's profound impact. The guilty verdict forces us all to confront our own role in the fragile dance of faith and betrayal.

Trust has been convicted, but the question remains: can humanity learn from its mistakes, or will we continue to misuse and misunderstand the very thing we put on trial?

The verdict sets a chilling precedent. Experts warn, with Trust convicted, humanity faces a moral and emotional reckoning. How do we function without Trust? We've just declared guilty the very thing that holds us together.

As the world digests the verdict, its implications are clear. Relationships falter as people hesitate to rely on one another. Businesses crumble under the weight of distrust. Faith wavers as congregations question whether Trust in God is any different from Trust in man. Even the $8 trillion restitution meant to provide closure only deepen divisions. Who will oversee its distribution? How can such an astronomical sum ever truly compensate for the emotional and spiritual wounds it seeks to address?

Some celebrate the justice delivered, while others question the wisdom of convicting an idea so integral to the human experience.

And somewhere, in the recesses of an indefinite prison, Trust sits silently, awaiting the day when its innocence might finally be proven. Perhaps humanity will one day realize that Trust was never the villain. And maybe, just maybe, it will one day be exonerated.

As the courthouse lights dim and the world moves on, questions remain: *If we cannot Trust, what hope remains for us all?*

CHAPTER 10

Not Guilty Verdict Declared

THIS IS IT! The moment we've all been waiting for. Everyone is on the edge of their seats. No one moves. No one breathes. Even time stands still, holding its breath, awaiting the verdict that will determine Trust's fate.

Trust looks restless, like he hasn't slept in ages. His swollen are eyes reminiscent of Rocky Balboa's fights with Apollo Creed. This trial pushed him to his breaking point. His head hangs as he scans the courtroom. No matter which way the verdict swings, Earnest Trust has accepted his fate. His hands fidget tirelessly as his cufflinks rattle against the table. It's impossible to hide the nerves flowing out of him.

The jury files in, everyone fixating on the foreperson as the jury takes their seats.

Judge Steele's voice breaks the anxious silence. "Has the jury reached a verdict?"

"We have, Your Honor." The foreperson states as she passes the verdict to the bailiff.

Judge Steele quickly scans the verdict and hands it back. "Very well. Would the defendant please rise? Please read the verdict."

The jury foreperson stands, her hands trembling as she gulps loudly, clutching the slip of paper that will forever alter the narrative of Trust's role in the human story. She clears her throat and delivers the verdict.

"On the charge of *fraud*, we find the defendant, Trust, *NOT GUILTY*. On the charge of *breach of contract*, we find the defendant, Trust, *NOT GUILTY.*"

The courtroom explodes with an overwhelming surge of applause, laughter, gasps, headshakes, and everything in between. A wave of relief, disbelief, and quiet joy sweeps throughout. A collective exhale ripples through the courtroom.

Trust takes a long, deep breath. He falls down in his chair, clenching his fists and pumping them up and down. Shield closes his eyes briefly. A quiet prayer of gratitude passes from his lips.

The prosecutor, Reed, stays seated. His jaw tenses then releases. His brows knit together, only to lift a second later, caught between a slow dance of doubt and determination. His eyes dart around the room, taking the moment in. A shaky exhale slips past his lips, barely noticeable, but it's there. His hands are interlocked as he taps his index fingers together slowly. Disappointment fuses with something deeper, perhaps relief.

Judge Steele's gavel slams with finality, commanding silence. "Ladies and gentlemen, the jury has rendered its verdict. Trust is acquitted of all charges. Trust, you're free to go. Court is adjourned."

As Judge Steele's gavel echoes fade, Trust stands. His presence glistens, brimming with confidence. He doesn't gloat. He doesn't celebrate. He just holds his head up high. Turning to the jury, he bows his head slightly in a gesture of gratitude that screams: "*Thank you for believing.*"

Shield stands outside the courthouse for a press conference. The cameras flash, reporters jostle for position, and the world awaits his comments for this historic moment.

Shield approaches the podium and adjusts the microphone. He pauses, clearing his throat and allowing the crowd to settle. "Ladies and gentlemen, today's verdict is not just a win for Trust. It is a win for humanity. It is a reminder that Trust remains an essential part of what it means to be human. We defended Trust because we believed him to be the cornerstone of love, connection, and faith. Without Trust, the world fractures into chaos, isolation, and despair.

"This trial has shown us something profound: Trust is not perfect; it was never meant to be. It is fragile, yes, but that's what makes it so powerful. When we choose to Trust, despite the risks, we open ourselves up to transformation, redemption, and love. Trust was never the villain. It was the prosecution's scapegoat for humanity's missteps, a victim of misplaced faith and false expectations. And he stood in defiance of the accusations.

"Today, the jury declared Trust innocent. But the real victory is not ours. It belongs to every person who dares to Trust again. It belongs to every soul who chooses faith over fear, love over cynicism, and hope over despair. But let's be clear: Trust isn't the hero of this story. Today's victory points to something greater, someone greater.

"During this trial, we proved the problem isn't Trust, but where we choose to place it. We've seen repeatedly that when Trust is placed in flawed people, fleeting ideas, or fragile systems, it inevitably fails. But when Trust is rightly placed in God, it becomes something more. God is not just worthy of your Trust. He is the very foundation of Trust. The Bible reminds us in Proverbs 3:5–6, *'Trust in the Lord with all your heart and lean not on your own understanding; in all your ways acknowledge him, and shall direct your paths.'*

"This isn't just a call to Trust God with the 'big things.' It's a call to entrust every aspect of your lives to him—your faith, your finances, your health, your relationships, your hurts, your pains, your doubts, your very existence. Because the truth is, he is already in control."

Shield's tone softens as he leans closer to the microphone, "Let's be honest. How often do we say we Trust God, claiming he is in control? But then, we try and control our own lives on our own terms, in our own ways? We cling to worry, doubt, and anxiety over the very things God is in control of. We stress and fear about our futures, our loved ones, our careers. We hold grudges, unwilling to forgive. We rely on our own strength instead of surrendering to His.

"Today, I challenge you to let go of that illusion of control. The God who created you is not distant or uncaring. He is deeply invested in your life. He longs for you to Trust him with everything, not just the parts you're willing to surrender. And the beauty of it all is that Trusting God isn't blind faith. It's the most reasonable and secure thing you can do. Because God has already proven his trustworthiness in the most profound way—through Jesus Christ."

Shield pauses, allowing the moment to sink in. "Jesus Himself said: *'I am the way, the truth, and the life. No one comes to the Father except through me'* (John 14:6). This isn't a statement, it's an invitation. Through Jesus, God demonstrated the depth of his love and the extent of his trustworthiness. While we were still sinners, even enemies of God, Christ died for us. The Cross is the ultimate evidence that God is worthy of your Trust. Accepting Jesus as Lord and placing your trust in him is without question, the most unfair deal humanity has ever been offered.

"Consider the terms of this transaction, this divine exchange. God says, 'I will do everything. I will bridge the gap between your brokenness and my holiness. I will bear the penalty for your sin, endure the wrath meant for you, and offer you eternal life. All for free. All you have to do is Trust me.'

"In human context, such an offer is unthinkable. Imagine someone offering to pay off your debts, heal your wounds, and secure your future, all while asking for nothing in return except your belief, Trust, faith. It defies all logic and reason. It exceeds generosity and leaves no room for reciprocity.

"If we're honest, this feels impossibly simple, doesn't it? We live in a world where nothing comes free, where every deal has strings attached, and where Trust is often met with betrayal. The idea that God would do everything for us and ask only for our faith in return seems . . . unfair. And it is. It's unfair in the best way possible. When we truly grasp the unfairness of this deal, it changes everything. It humbles us. It silences our pride and self-sufficiency. It reminds us that our salvation is not something we earn, but something we receive.

"If you've ever doubted whether God loves you, whether he can truly be Trusted, or whether you are worthy of his grace, look to the Cross. It is the ultimate evidence that God is not only Trustworthy but abundantly so. And the most amazing part is that this deal is still on the table. All he asks is that you believe, that you Trust him.

"Today's verdict is more than a victory for Trust. It's a wake-up call for all of us, a reminder that Trust, when placed in the wrong hands, leads to heartbreak and pain. But when placed in God, it becomes the bridge to hope, healing, and redemption. This verdict is a win for every person who has ever been betrayed, every soul who has ever doubted, and every heart that longs for something greater.

"So, I challenge everyone listening. Let this verdict be the beginning of a new chapter in your life, a chapter where you entrust everything to God. Because when you do, you'll find that Trust is far from a liability. It is the key to the abundant life God has promised." Shield pauses one final time. "Thank you. And to God be the glory."

Outside the courthouse, a crowd of reporters swarms the steps, microphones extended like weapons of curiosity. Reed emerges with an uncharacteristically subdued expression. His lips are pursed together, his eyebrows are pulled tight, his head tilts slightly down. He fought with ferocity, armed with evidence and logic. And yet, he can't shake the thought: "*What if I've been wrong all along?*"

The crowd hushes as he approaches the podium. "Ladies and gentlemen, today's verdict marks the end of one chapter and the beginning of another. I stand before you, not as a prosecutor, but as a man deeply changed. I argued with everything that Trust was guilty. I believed it. But throughout the course of this trial, something happened. I listened. Not just to the evidence, but to my own heart.

"Trust is innocent, and while this was not the outcome I hoped for, I must admit . . . I believe it is the right one."

Surprised commotion ripples through the crowd. Reed raises his hand. "Throughout this trial, I approached Trust as a skeptic, maybe even an accuser. I presented witnesses and evidence to prove that Trust was unreliable, dangerous, and harmful. And yet, as the defense presented their case, I found myself . . . challenged. Not just as a prosecutor, but as a man.

"Dr. Lionheart spoke of humanity's tendency to put God in the dock, to judge him from our limited perspective. And I realized that's exactly what I've been doing, not just in this trial, but in my own life. I've spent years questioning God's goodness, blaming him for suffering, and refusing to Trust in him. But something shifted. As I listened to the defense's argument for Trust, I began to see my problem wasn't with Trust, it was with where I had placed it. I had Trusted in my own intellect, my own strength, my own judgment. And I had failed to see that true Trust, rightly placed in God, is not a gamble; it is a lifeline."

Reed pauses, his voice trembling. "As I stand here today, I no longer see God as distant or untrustworthy. I see him as the ultimate source of hope and redemption. And I choose—publicly, here and now—to place my Trust in Him. I've heard the challenge, the call to something more. Today, I choose to place my Trust in something greater, someone greater. I choose to believe that redemption is possible, not just for Trust, but for all of us."

The crowd stands stunned. Open mouths and wide eyes infiltrate the crowd. Cameras furiously click, trying to capture the moment of raw vulnerability.

Reed steps back, filled with a peace that has eluded him for years. "Thank you. That's all for now."

The world erupts as the jury declares Trust not guilty. Relief, reflection, and a sense of cautious optimism wash over social media, with users celebrating the verdict as a win for humanity and hope.

Social media is a firestorm of heartfelt posts about redemption and restoration. The hashtag *#TrustWins* trends immediately as users share stories of times when they had been betrayed but still found healing through renewed Trust. "#TrustWins because, without it, how do we live, love, or hope?" writes one user, her post accompanied by a wedding day photo.

Clips from the courtroom's press conferences circulate like wildfire. The prosecutor's admission of faith after the trial strikes a chord with millions, creating viral moments of unity and introspection. "This trial didn't just exonerate Trust, it exonerated something inside me," he said, prompting hashtags like #TrustRestored and #FaithInGod.

Meanwhile, Shield's press conference becomes a symbol of resilience and faith as he credited God for delivering the victory. A line from his speech, "Hope cannot exist without Trust," becomes an anthem for online movements calling for renewed connection and forgiveness. Trending Hashtags for the Innocent Verdict break out across social media.

1. *#TrustWins*: The definitive hashtag for the verdict, symbolizing hope and the power of restored trust.

2. *#FaithInTrust*: A celebratory hashtag used by those who see the verdict as a testament to Trust's role in humanity's survival.

3. *#TrustRestored*: A hopeful tag encouraging people to rebuild bridges and rekindle their faith in others.

4. *#VictoryForTrust*: Used to celebrate the defense's monumental win.

5. *#TheCaseForHope*: Inspired by the defense's argument that Trust is essential for love, faith, and redemption.

6. *#FaithInGod*: A spiritual hashtag tied to the prosecutor's surprising change of heart after the trial.

The verdict sends shockwaves around the globe. "No justice, no peace," becomes a rallying cry with protestors lining the streets all around the country, outraged by the not-guilty verdict. #Rigged and #BoughtandPaidFor trend on social media in opposition to the hope-inspired hashtags and celebrations. Various news media outlets praise the verdict while several others take to the airwaves to condemn this egregious betrayal by the jury. One side is elated, relieved, proclaiming justice has been served. And other side is heated, overwhelmed with disgust at the injustice. Much like the great toilet paper debate, it's impossible to please everyone.

While the world outside wrestles with the verdict, a quiet shift takes place with conversations about Trust, faith, and forgiveness sweeping through homes, workplaces, and places of worship. People who had long guarded their hearts consider the possibility of Trusting again, not blindly, but with discernment. Churches report an influx of new attendees, many of whom cite the trial as the catalyst for their spiritual awakening. Families estranged by betrayal take hesitant steps toward reconciliation. And individuals burdened by doubt find themselves daring to hope again.

But one thing is certain, the trial of Trust has forever changed how we see the fragile yet vital force that binds us all together.

With the courtroom cleared and the verdict rendered, the trial of Trust will be the subject of endless debates. But the voices of the jury remain largely a mystery. Until now.

Standing across from Juror Seven in an isolated corner on the courthouse steps, a middle-aged reporter leans in, ready to capture the essence of what swayed the jury.

Reporter: "Thank you for agreeing to speak with us. The trial has captivated millions, but what people are really curious to know is how the jury came to its decision. Could you walk us through your thought process?"

Juror Seven: [Pausing, exhaling deeply] "It wasn't an easy decision, that's for sure. Trust, well, it's complicated, isn't it? At the beginning of the trial, I was skeptical. I mean, look at all the evidence the prosecution presented. The Bernie Madoff scandal, the stories of betrayal, broken promises, and pain. It all felt so overwhelming, so damning, and so personal. For a while, I was convinced they were right. Trust seemed guilty of fraud and breach of contract. How could it not be?"

Reporter: "What changed your mind?"

Juror Seven: "It wasn't one thing; it was the sum of everything. If I had to pinpoint it, I would say it was the defense's ability to contextualize the accusations. They didn't deny that Trust is fragile or that it gets broken, they embraced that. But they reframed it. They showed us that Trust wasn't the villain here.

"For example, the story of James Harrison hit me hard. Here was a man who lost everything during a horrific hurricane, and yet he never stopped Trusting in God. That kind of faith is rare, and it made me wonder: If he could Trust in the face of unimaginable suffering, maybe Trust wasn't the problem. Maybe it was about where we place it."

Reporter: "Did any other testimony stand out to you?"

Juror Seven: "Oh, absolutely. Dr. Malcolm Lionheart was . . . well, I'm still reeling from his testimony. When he said that humanity puts God in the dock as if we're the judge and he's the defendant, it really hit home. It made me realize how much we project our pain and disappointment onto God, blaming him for things that aren't his fault.

"And then there was the Cross. The defense called it the ultimate evidence of God's Trustworthiness, and I couldn't argue with that. That God would sacrifice his own Son for us—that's Trust in its purest, most selfless form. It made me think: If God Trusts us enough to give us free will, knowing we'll misuse it, maybe we should reconsider how we see Trust."

Reporter: "Was there a moment of doubt? Did the prosecution's arguments linger in your mind?"

Juror Seven: [Nodding] "Oh, absolutely. The prosecution's closing argument was powerful. They laid out the pain caused by misplaced Trust, broken relationships, institutional failures, and tied it all back to Trust as a defendant. It was hard not to be swayed by the weight of their evidence.

"But then the defense flipped it. They argued that Trust was the victim in all of it—misused, misunderstood, and unfairly blamed. It made me see the prosecution's evidence in a new light. Yes, people have suffered because of broken Trust, but the fault lies with those who abuse and betray him, not with Trust itself."

Reporter: "What about the artifacts and historical evidence presented by the defense? Did that influence your decision?"

Juror Seven: "100 percent. The defense's use of historical evidence was brilliant. The Foundation Stone tied Abraham's story to a tangible, real-world location. The Babylonian bricks and artifacts tied Shadrach, Meshach, and Abed-Nego to historical events. And Josephus's writings about Jesus really made an impact. I couldn't help but examine and reflect on the significance of our currency, something we all use every day. And even I take for granted the words etched on every bill, every coin, 'In God We Trust.' There was no denying its impact on our nation's identity.

"But really, it was the Cross that sealed it for me. The defense framed it not just as a religious symbol but as evidence of God's ultimate Trustworthiness. They argued that the Cross proved God's willingness to bear the consequences of human sin and betrayal. That was a game-changer."

Reporter: "So, what would you say to those who disagree with the verdict?"

Juror Seven: [Leaning forward] "I'd say this: Don't dismiss Trust because it's been misused or broken in the past. That's not Trust's fault, it's ours. And don't confuse the failings of people or institutions with the failings of Trust itself. Trust is what allows us to love, to hope, to build relationships. Without Trust, we're just isolated, suspicious, and bitter. And while it's easy to point fingers when things go wrong, this trial taught me that the real question isn't whether Trust is guilty, it's whether we're willing to give it another chance."

Reporter: "One last question. Do you think the verdict will change how people see Trust?"

Juror Seven: [Smiling] "I sure hope so. Trust is risky, sure. But Trust is essential. Without Trust, we have no connection, no progress, no faith. This trial reminded me that Trust can change everything. I just hope others see that too."

As Juror Seven walks away, their words linger, a testament to the transformational power of the trial. The verdict isn't just about Trust's guilt or innocence; it is a call for humanity to reconsider its own role in the delicate balance of faith and relationships. Trust has been vindicated, but the true victory rests in the hearts of those willing to Trust again.

Trust walks alone, radiant. He stops in front of the courthouse window, staring out at the world he was accused of betraying. "Vindication," he whispers, the word heavy with relief. "But the work is far from over." As Trust bursts forth from the courthouse doors, the sunlight warms his face. His path is clear. To continue his quiet, life-changing work in the hearts of those willing to believe. Not in perfection, but in redemption.

For the jury, the trial is over. And for humanity, the question remains: *"Now that Trust is innocent, what will we do with it?"*

As the trial closes and the chapter ends, readers are invited to reflect on their own verdict: *Trust has been declared innocent, but what does that mean for you? What role does Trust play in your life? Are there areas you have misplaced Trust, and where might you place your Trust anew? Will you dare to Trust again?*

Trust stands, ready and willing—ready to walk in lockstep beside you, into a future filled with hope. And perhaps, so are we.

CHAPTER 11

The Challenge, A Call to Trust

THE COURTROOM IS CLOSED NOW. The jury has deliberated, the verdict has been delivered, and the trial of Trust is over. Let's talk, you and me. Yes, you, the reader still holding this book, flipping through its pages. You've journeyed through the prosecution's scorching allegations, witnessed the defense's fiery rebuttals, and perhaps found yourself somewhere in between. But now, it's personal.

For you, this story is just beginning. Because the truth about Trust isn't confined to a book, or a courtroom trial, or the court of public opinion. It's not even captured in a single verdict. It is a decision each one of us makes daily, moment by moment.

And now the decision lies in your hands.

Trust isn't just on trial in this book; it's on trial in your life. This entire trial has been about you. It's about whether you'll step into the redeeming, abundant, life-altering reality of fully entrusting every part of your existence to God.

The question isn't just whether Trust is guilty or innocent; it's whether you're willing to take a stand and place your Trust where it really belongs—in the hands of the only one who is truly trustworthy.

Before we dive into these personal challenges, I'd like to share something personal with you: Writing this book wasn't an academic exercise or a creative endeavor. It was born out of my own journey—a journey filled with doubt, pain, and, ultimately, reflection and revelation. Before I dare to ask you to jump in, allow me to share my personal testimony and my heart behind this book.

Childhood trauma taught me early on that the world is not a safe place. People fail you. Promises break. Love can twist into something unrecognizable. My ability to trust was fractured before it even had a chance to form.

What is your earliest childhood memory? Is it something happy? Something joyful? At least something positive? Well, mine is none of those things. My earliest childhood memory is sitting inside a child psychologist's office, playing with some toys, and speaking to the therapist about how my birth mother interacted with me inappropriately. I was confused. I didn't know why I was there. I just knew I wanted to be anywhere but there, and I certainly didn't want to talk about it. What three- to five-year-old talks about their feelings anyway?

Another time, a few years later, I remember getting woken up in the middle of the night and dragged out of my bed. I had a half-coherent, barely-eyes-open discussion with the cops about why my birth mother called them, explaining how she could hear me screaming in the middle of the night. And I proceeded to tell them I had long been asleep and was perfectly safe. I couldn't have been more than eight years old at the time.

Looking back on it, it's clear to me that my sense of security was shaken from a very young age. Children, especially young children, are innocent and their parents are supposed to protect them. And ultimately, this shook my foundations and my ability to fully trust things.

Luckily, my father protected me and so did my step-mom . . . who was truly my mom. It was my mom who brought me to church ever since I can remember. It was my mom who was always reading her Bible in the morning. It was my mom who was always taking me to church on Sunday mornings, Sunday nights, and Wednesday nights. It was always my mom. My dad came to church, but he was the typical CEO churchgoer—Christmas and Easter Only.

I feel like I gave my life to Jesus at a young age, eight or nine. I remember just believing that Jesus died for me and I needed to believe in him so I could have eternal life. I remember being baptized around nine or ten and then again at even eleven or twelve as I further understood the significance as I got older.

Part of my coming to know God and the person of Jesus Christ came from being scared. I was afraid of ending up in hell, separated from my mom and God himself. I was afraid of being left behind. To be honest, I've felt those same feelings in adulthood. God was the answer, and that's why I believed in him. But Jesus was also security for me. Because of the evil ever-present in the world, I realize as an adult that my sense of security was compromised. And it truly impacted my ability to trust, the older I've gotten. I certainly had insecurities and trust issues, which reared their ugly head from time to time. And they've continued to bleed into other areas of my life.

When I reached the age of sixteen, I wasn't really walking with the Lord. I was having sex, partying with friends, drinking. I eventually got my girlfriend, now wife of almost twenty years, pregnant six months after turning eighteen. I joined the Navy, and we had our first child just after I turned the wise age of nineteen. The moment I saw my son, I was overwhelmed with emotion. I cried like a baby and just sat there, thinking in the recesses of my mind, wondering, "What did I ever do to deserve this?" Jesus blessed me with something indescribable and it changed my life—forever. It pointed me back to Jesus.

But it wasn't for a few more years before I got my life back on track and pointed in the direction of Jesus. My family and I moved to Virginia when I was about twenty-two. We found a church there and I started going to counseling with a great pastor. It was there I felt Jesus reach out and touch me, leading to overwhelming tears and a reminder that Jesus never left—I did.

What's truly amazing about Jesus is that he is always there. He never leaves you or forsakes you. He is right there, waiting for you, even when you decide to walk your own path. Even when you aren't faithful, he always is. Even when you aren't in fellowship with Him. I think about the trials and issues I ran into during the times I was not in fellowship with God, and it was incredibly more difficult. I made a lot of selfish and foolish decisions.

Before God, I was a scared and insecure little boy, attempting to please those around me, wanting to be liked, being the class clown, and needing to be the best, the smartest, the most talented. I was so unsure of who I was, and I was only looking out for myself. I was so unsure of who was really there protecting me. It was extremely difficult to trust much of anyone besides my parents.

But now, I've fully entrusted my life to Jesus and surrendered my life in service to Him. I'm secure and confident. I'm less concerned with what anyone thinks of me and more concerned with accomplishing God's will in my life. God's fingerprints are all over my life. I see his continual blessings and fruit in my life. He has revealed and continues to reveal himself to me in the most amazing and powerful ways.

I want to hear those words, "Well done, good and faithful servant, enter into the joy of the Lord." I want to represent Jesus the right way. The overarching theme I see over and over again throughout the Bible is that God blesses his children—even when they don't see it, even when they don't acknowledge it, even when they don't deserve it. And it resonates even more with me as a parent of six.

If I'm honest, I still struggle with that confidence and that security, and part of that is probably because of childhood trauma. It's not me questioning Jesus or his work on the cross or even his resurrection. The question I struggle with is, "Am I worthy to be saved?" . . . and I'm not, no one is. I know that. But then it spirals into, "Did I say the prayer correctly? Does my doubt mean I'm not saved?" Like, I remember saying the prayer. Several times, I prayed that prayer, dedicating and rededicating my life, and I meant it every time. I gave my life over to the Lord many times.

And then I had an epiphany: you either believe him or you don't. When Jesus says, "Confess with your mouth the Lord Jesus and believe in your heart that God raised him from the dead you will be saved," (Romans 10:9) that is a mic drop moment! End all, be all. You either believe the work Jesus did AND you believe the words written and spoken of how to receive salvation, or you don't. It's as simple as that.

You have to come to the realization that everything Jesus said and did was historically accurate, true, and factual. With all the proof we have, we know God's word and the Bible are true. Everything God says will, in fact, come to pass. Jesus is the True and Faithful witness. We are the ones who are untrustworthy and faithless.

For years, I thought I could control certain aspects of my life: my circumstances, my relationships, my finances, my future. And I kept coming up short, left feeling broken.

I didn't fully trust God—not with my finances, my health, or even my own questions and doubts. I held onto the "what-ifs," clutching my fears like they were life preservers, all the while sinking deeper. I've guarded my heart, built up walls, and isolated myself, fearing the pain of shattered trust. I'd convinced myself that I could handle things, that I had some semblance of control of my life. And so I latched onto that, tightly. If I could just control what I could control, then I wouldn't have to bother God. We would be like partners. It's not that I didn't think God couldn't manage or control aspects of my life; I was more so convinced I didn't need to bother God with my problems. I could manage just fine.

Spoiler alert: I couldn't.

When you try to control things beyond your control, it leads to stress, anxiety, worry, etc. You were never meant to shoulder the load, to control the uncontrollable, to carry the burden, or to do *just* fine. God's desire is for us to live life and more abundantly.

Is doing "just fine" living an abundant life? Does that sound like thriving? Or just surviving?

It was through writing my testimony that the Holy Spirit revealed the truth: I wasn't in control, I never have been, and more importantly, I never will be. And that's okay because God is. He's always been there, even when I wasn't faithful. He's always been trustworthy, even when I doubted. Trusting God isn't about having all the answers. It's about knowing the one who does.

The turning point was simple. Did I truly believe? *You can't believe some things in the Bible while being uncertain of the others. I had to decide whether I really believed the Bible and what God said or not.*

When God says, "Confess with your mouth the Lord Jesus and believe in your heart that God raised him from the dead, you will be saved" (Romans 10:9), do I believe that? If I believe Jesus is who he says he is, if I believe his words that the Bible is true, then I should have the utmost confidence that I can trust him with everything.

And so, the challenge begins.

The Challenge: A Call to Fully Entrust Every Aspect of Your Life to God

So, here's the deal. I'm not asking you to "sort of" trust God. No halfway measures. This is a full-send kind of challenge. God doesn't ask for part of your trust; he asks for all of it. This isn't about dipping your toes into faith; it's about diving headfirst into the deep end, knowing he will hold you up.

And yeah, it's scary. Trusting God means surrendering control, and let's be honest, that's terrifying. But it's also freeing.

Let's break it down.

1. *Trust God with Your Entire Life*

Your life is like a priceless vase perched on the edge of a wobbly table. You can try to hold it steadily, but your hands are shaky. God, on the other hand, is the craftsman who made the vase. He knows every curve, every flaw, every intricate design. When you trust him, you're not giving up control, you're giving it back to the one who had it all along.

Think about it. God created the universe. He spoke stars into existence and formed you in your mother's womb. If he can handle the cosmos, don't you think he can handle your life?

But here's the catch, trusting God means surrendering control. It means saying, "Lord, I can't do this on my own. I need you."

Challenge: Take a moment right now. Reflect on the areas of your life where you've held back from God. Is it your career? Your relationships? Your dreams? Write them down. Then, one by one, surrender them to Him.

2. *Trust God* with *Your Finances*

Ah, money, the universal panic button. Let's be honest, money is one of the hardest areas to trust God. We think, "What if I don't have enough? What if I lose my job? What if an emergency comes up?" But here's the truth: *God owns it all.*

"The earth is the Lord's, and everything in it" (Psalm 24:1). Your paycheck? That's his provision. Your savings? His blessing. Your tithe? An act of trust.

Challenge: If you've been holding back on tithing or giving, take the step of faith. Give generously, not because God needs your money but because he deserves your trust.

3. *Trust God with Your Health*

How often do we think, "I'm healthy because I eat right, exercise, and take care of myself? I drink smoothies that taste like regret." While those things are important, they are not ultimate. Your next breath is a gift from God. Your heartbeat is sustained by his hand.

Challenge: Entrust your health to God. Pray over your body, not just for healing when you're sick but for strength, energy, and the ability to serve him when you're well.

4. *Trust God with Your Relationships*

We've all been hurt by people—betrayed, abandoned, or let down. And those wounds make it hard to trust again. But here's the thing, God is the healer of broken relationships.

Challenge: Bring your relationships to God—your spouse, your children, your friends, even your enemies. Ask him to guide you, to heal what's broken, and to help you forgive as he forgave you.

5. *Trust* God *with Your Forgiveness*

Forgiveness isn't easy. As the old saying goes, "Fool me once, shame on you. Fool me twice, shame on me." It feels unfair, like letting someone off the hook. But forgiveness isn't about excusing the offense; it's about freeing yourself from its grip.

Challenge: Think of someone you need to forgive. Write their name down. Then, pray over them and the situation. Ask God to help you release the bitterness and extend the same grace he's given you.

Here's the glorious truth of it all: Trusting God begins and ends with Jesus. He is God, and he has every right to tell us how and in what manner to get him. And the answer is Jesus.

Jesus says, *"I am the way, the truth, and the life. No one comes to the father except through me" (John 14:6).* This is the law of affirmation. By Jesus affirming he is the only way to God, he doesn't then need to list all the ways that don't lead to God. Jesus is the bridge between our brokenness and God's holiness.

Let's be real: Accepting Jesus as Lord isn't just a leap of faith, it's the most unfair deal you'll ever make. It's ridiculously unfair.

He says, "I will do everything. I'll bear your sin, your shame, your guilt. All I ask is that you trust me."

Jesus doesn't just ask for your trust. He's earned it. Through the Cross, he proved that no one loves you more, fights for you harder, or deserves your trust more fully.

Challenge: If you haven't already, make the decision to follow Jesus. Confess with your mouth that he is Lord. By confessing Jesus as Lord, you are also admitting that you are not. Believe in your heart that God raised him from the dead, and watch as he transforms your life.

If there's one thing I've learned, it's this: *God is trustworthy.* He doesn't promise an easy life, but he promises a meaningful one—a life filled with his presence, his peace, his promises, and his purpose.

Trust isn't just a concept or a defendant in a trial. Trust isn't just about belief. It's about action. It's about saying, "Lord, I don't understand everything, but I trust you with everything."

And when you choose to place your trust in God, you're not just finding security, you're finding life itself—abundant life.

The challenge is before you. The choice is yours. Will you trust Him?

If you're ready to take the step of faith, pray this prayer: "Lord, I confess that I've tried to control my life instead of trusting you. I've held back my finances, my health, my relationships, my forgiveness, and my heart.

Today, I surrender it all to you. I place my trust in Jesus as my Lord and Savior. Help me to walk in faith, knowing that you are good, you are in control, and you are enough. Amen."

This is your moment. The trial has ended. The verdict is emphatically clear: God is trustworthy. Now, it's time to live like it.

Choose Trust. Choose life. Choose God!

Bibliography

Bible Hub.com. 4100. *pisteuó*. Accessed December 31, 2024. https://biblehub.com/greek/4100.htm.

Josephus, Flavius. *Antiquities of the Jews, Book* 18, *Chapter* 3, *Section* 3. Translated by Louis H. Feldman. Loeb Classical Library. Cambridge, MA:: Harvard University Press, 1986.

Lewis, C. S. *A Mind Awake: An Anthology of C. S. Lewis.* San Francisco: HarperOne, 2003.

———. *A Mind Awake: An Anthology of C. S. Lewis.* San Francisco: HarperOne, 2003.

———. *God in the Dock: Essays on Theology and Ethics.* Grand Rapids: William B. Eerdmans, 1970.

———. *Mere Chritianity.* London: William Collins, 2012.

———. *The Joyful Christian.* NewYork: Macmillan, 1977.

———. *The Problem of Pain.* London: The Centenary, 1940.

Merriam-Webster.com Dictionary. *s. v.* "*confidence*". Accessed December 31, 2024. https://www.merriam-webster.com/dictionary/confidence.

———. *s. v.* "*entrusting*". Accessed December 31, 2024. https://www.merriam-webster.com/dictionary/entrusting.

———. *s. v.* "*trust*". Accessed December 31, 2024. https://www.merriam-webster.com/dictionary/trust.